Ecstas

"BLAIR, WHY WON'T YOU?" HE WHISPERED AGAINST HER SKIN.

"I can't, Mitch," she answered softly. "Please don't ask me to. I can't."

"I don't know what to say, Blair." His voice was a dry whisper. "I suddenly feel seventeen again in the backseat of a car."

Her voice was as dry as his and as brittle. "Out with one of the uninhibited girls in school? Is that it?"

He paused and lifted one brow at her. "No." He gave a short laugh. "Those weren't the ones who always stopped me; it was the nice inhibited ones like you. How do you cut your emotions off like that?"

Her darkened yes locked on his. "Mitch, you give me too much credit, or not enough, I don't know which. And I don't know that it matters. I am not inhibited, I am merely a woman who will not make love with a man who is little more than a stranger to her."

He was silent a moment, then said, "Desire makes strangers—friends, don't you think?"

"Yes. Then when it's gone, burned up, burned out, the friends are strangers again."

A CANDLELIGHT ECSTASY ROMANCE ®

WINDSONG

Jo Calloway

A CANDLELIGHT ECSTASY ROMANCE ®

Published by
Dell Publishing Co., Inc.
1 Dag Hammarskjold Plaza
New York, New York 10017

Dell ® TM 681510, Dell Publishing Co., Inc.

Candlelight Ecstasy Romance®, 1,203,540, is a registered
trademark of
Dell Publishing Co., Inc.,
New York, New York.

ISBN: 0-440-19495-4

Printed in the United States of America
First printing—November 1983

To Our Readers:

We have been delighted with your enthusiastic response to Candlelight Ecstasy Romances®, and we thank you for the interest you have shown in this exciting series.

In the upcoming months we will continue to present the distinctive sensuous love stories you have come to expect only from Ecstasy. We look forward to bringing you many more books from your favorite authors and also the very finest work from new authors of contemporary romantic fiction.

As always, we are striving to present the unique, absorbing love stories that you enjoy most—books that are more than ordinary romance.

Your suggestions and comments are always welcome. Please write to us at the address below.

Sincerely,

The Editors
Candlelight Romances
1 Dag Hammarskjold Plaza
New York, New York 10017

CHAPTER ONE

She leaned her arms on the desk, rested her face in her hands, and sighed. What a week! What an awful week. Her lips twisted in a forlorn grin and she said aloud, "Thank God for Friday." Her eyes rolled upward. "That goes double this week," she added as she rubbed one side of her forehead with long tapered fingers.

Without moving her head she scanned the office. Files were strewn everywhere—on the desktop, on the file cabinet, on the table, on the bookcase, in the bookcase. She closed her eyes tightly. She would have to muster up more strength than she had at the moment to open her attaché case. She was sure with the mess of papers inside it would look like the last five folders had participated in a pulp orgy. She had grabbed and yanked, fought and argued for five full days, but now it was over.

The intercom beeped and she leaned over slightly

and pressed the button. Before Lynn Mathison, her legal secretary, could speak, she whispered low into the speaker, "Tell me, Lynn, why does anybody get married?" Her voice dropped a full octave and she added, "All perspective brides and grooms should be forced to come look at my office. It should be a court order."

Lynn laughed. "Blair, I hate to tell you this, but there's a call on line one from a man who won't give his name, but insists on speaking with you. I'm putting it mildly when I say he sounds excited."

Still speaking in mockingly low tones, Blair answered, "Tell him I've gone for the day—no, tell him I've gone for the weekend. An excited male is the last thing I need on this particular Friday." She smiled suddenly. "But tell him to call back Monday."

"All right, Blair. I'll be in there shortly to start with the files."

Blair released the button and watched the blinking light as line one stopped flashing. She knew her efficient assistant was taking care of the caller.

Then suddenly the light began blinking again and immediately the intercom beeped. She pressed, but before she could say anything, Lynn, sounding a bit excited herself, said, "Blair, maybe you had better talk with him. He's really upset. He said if he didn't speak with you that you would find your own blankety-blank in court next week!"

"Did he actually say blankety-blank?" Blair's back straightened.

"No. I was just trying to soften the message."

Blair inhaled deeply. "Well, you reply to Mr. Excited that my blankety-blank has been in court all

10

this week so it's quite familiar with the hard seats and would look forward to meeting him there next week. And, Lynn, don't soften the message. And then hang up and grab your purse. Before he calls back we'll have escaped."

This time when she released the intercom she bolted from her chair, opened the bottom drawer of her desk, and removed her purse. When the light on line one went off she stood in the reception room of the office suite.

Lynn, a short thin attractive woman of twenty-seven, looked up from behind her desk and shook her head. "That is one mad man. I'm telling you, Blair, he's furious."

"Well, let's get out of here before he calls back. You know, he's probably one of the emancipated men from our week's work." Her brows raised. "Was he drunk?"

Lynn inhaled deeply and rose quickly from her chair. "No, I don't think so, but I really couldn't tell."

"Well, he probably was. This has happened before, so don't worry about it." She made quick little motions with her hand. "Let's go. Anybody that excited will no doubt dial again."

Lynn joined her, saying, "What about the mess here?"

Blair gave a quick shake of her head. "It'll probably still be here Monday. I don't think it will clean itself up, and the good fairy of cleanliness wouldn't touch it with a mile-long pole." She opened the door and held it while Lynn walked out first, then followed, pausing to lock up. Through the glass she

11

could see the light on the telephone flashing. She raised her brows and pointed, saying over to Lynn, "See there, what did I tell you?"

Lynn murmured low, "I hope he cools down by Monday. I never thought about it before, but being in the divorce business could be dangerous. My Lord, I could be sitting there at my desk, doing my work, and be wiped out the next minute by some irate person."

Blair looked over with a dancing light in her eyes. "Lynn, I'm sorry I encouraged you to read *The Godfather*. You haven't been quite the same since."

Lynn sighed. "Well, it gives a person something to think about . . . for sure."

Blair laughed cheerily. "Don't think about it. Go on home and love your husband and kiss your children. Have a good weekend."

Lynn laughed. "I couldn't do that. Terry would probably think I'm having an affair. What are you going to do this weekend, Blair?" she inquired as they moved toward the parking lot.

"Oh, I'm going to have a very quiet, leisurely time. I'm going out with Wayne tomorrow night, but otherwise I'm going to lie around, doing nothing, recuperating from all my divorces."

"See you Monday." Lynn smiled, parting to walk to another section of the parking lot.

Blair Bennett smiled a farewell, then moved thoughtfully in the direction of her car. She walked smoothly and with confidence. A barefoot five-five, she always wore three-inch heels to court so that her male counterparts didn't have to look so far down their noses to see her. Her wide eyes were big and dark bluish-green, her crisp curly hair a soft honey blond. A natural flush in her cheeks gave her a look of health, even following a tiring week like the one just ending.

She walked abstractedly to the car, her full, shapely lips pinched tight as she tried to recover her wits. No matter how hard she tried, sometimes her work got to her.

She slid into the car, started the motor, and drove slowly to the street where she stopped to look for oncoming traffic. Her gaze froze as she glanced back for a final farewell to her office. There stood a man at the door, peering through the glass, his hands on the sides of his face like horse blinders.

She eyed him keenly a moment from the distance. He was very tall and dark-haired. That was all she could tell from where she sat—and she didn't want a closer look. Inhaling deeply, she pulled into the street and drove off at a rapid speed. His stance relayed to her that he was the unnamed caller of minutes ago. His entire body emitted anger.

She was quite baffled why anyone would be upset with her. In each case she had only done what she was retained to do. But she wasn't going to think about it and allow unwelcomed worry to ruin her days of rest and relaxation. No, indeed, she'd worked too hard this week.

The next morning, after a restful night's sleep, she pulled on short strapless terry-cloth rompers, picked up the morning paper, and went outside to the patio where she stretched out on her chaise longue. For a few minutes she watched her neighbor's oversize

German shepherd run along the lawn then stop and burrow her nose in the low grass in fast chase after an escaping insect. A few moments passed and she saw the dog's head shoot up with a sudden low howl filling the air. Blair laughed aloud and shook her head. Poor Duchess. That dog was never going to learn not to chase bees. The German shepherd's nose had not been normal size since spring came to Virginia and the clover and bees had miraculously appeared, much to the dog's delight—and dismay.

The door opened on the patio next to Blair's and a woman in a cotton print robe shot out. She looked over to Blair, then down to her still whimpering monster of a dog. "Blair," she called out, "did you see what happened to Duchess?"

Blair hid her amusement. "I think a bee stung her on the nose," she called back over the thirty-foot space separating the two backyards. Smiling brightly, she watched Lana Harris bound out onto the lawn, her high squeaky voice ringing out to console her pet. "Oh, Duchess, you bad girl. When are you going to learn to leave those bees alone? Be still so I can get the stinger out of your nose."

After Lana returned to the house, Duchess came over to Blair's patio, her head drooped, her bushy tail between her hind legs. She nudged Blair on the leg with her swelling nose.

"Poor Duchess," Blair said in a consoling tone, rubbing the dog's head between the ears. "You have such a hard time. Why don't you lie down here beside me and I'll protect you against those buzzing monsters."

The dog seemed to just melt in a big hairy blob on

the concrete floor beside the lounge chair and Blair opened the morning paper.

With Duchess settled, she leaned back and lost herself in the print. Her gaze was drawn to the list of divorces granted during the past week in the quarterly session of the circuit court. She counted them. One hundred and eleven. Then she counted again. Thirty-eight. Her own list of clients totaled thirty-eight. More than any other attorney in the city.

Except for her slight feelings of despair that her speciality had developed in civil cases such as divorce, she was proud of her overall accomplishments. She had become known as the "Woman's Lawyer." Though she really hadn't intended for it to turn out like this, she couldn't argue with the reputation or monetary success it had gained her.

At twenty-nine she was self-sufficient, and with all she had seen and heard during the past three years in practice she felt sure she would remain that way.

She lowered her paper, lifted a glass of tomato juice from the table beside the lounge, and languidly looked up at the magnificent April morning sky. She yawned deeply and carried into her lungs the fresh scent, sweet and simple, of clover and early blooming flowers. She yawned and stretched again, thinking she would merely laze the day away. The past week had tired her both physically and mentally.

Allowing the paper to fall on her chest, she melted back against the soft cushion and closed her eyes. In a matter of moments she was asleep. There was not a sound in the entire neighborhood, and on her covered patio just the soft breathing sounds of a woman and the sleeping beast beside her.

Then suddenly the serene silence was shattered. Duchess was on her feet barking and growling at the top of her lungs, every hair on her neck and back bristling a warning.

Blair jerked up in a flash, her eyes wide with surprise, wildly looking first at the ferocious dog, then upward to the source of the sudden upheaval on her patio. There, standing at the edge of the concrete, was a tall dark-haired man with a hard-looking jaw and piercing pale eyes. "I would appreciate it," he said gruffly, "if you would call off your dog."

"What are you doing on my patio!" she exclaimed.

"Well, after your week's work it seems I don't have anywhere else to go! Now, will you call off the dog." He stiffened as Duchess began to edge in his direction, still barking and growling with every breath.

"Come back, Duchess," Blair called, and immediately the dog stopped and turned back in her direction. "Now, what do you want?" she exclaimed loudly over the continuous growl. "Hush, Duchess," she said firmly, grabbing the dog's collar.

The intruder inhaled slowly, looking at Duchess. "What's wrong with that dog's nose?" he said while exhaling. "Biggest nose I've ever seen on a German shepherd."

"What's wrong with her nose is none of your business," Blair returned smartly. "And I would like to know just exactly what your business happens to be. Why are you trespassing on my property?"

"You are Blair Bennett, aren't you?" he returned sourly.

"Yes, I am."

"The attorney?" he snarled.

"That's right," she said coolly. In that instant she knew she had not seen many men as angry, nor as handsome, as the man standing on her patio.

"Do you know what you've done!"

"No," she said in her most controlled tone. "Why don't you tell me. But please be brief. I am but one-half second away from calling the police and having you removed from my property."

Both of his hands jerked outward in quick, angry little gestures. "Go ahead!" he yelled over Duchess's second spurt of barking. "I would expect you to do something like that! Feel free, call the police! Call the highway patrol! Call out the National Guard! Do whatever you feel you must in your heart!" Suddenly his voice softened with a flooding sarcasm. "But, then, you don't have a heart, do you?"

She matched his sudden sarcasm. "I have something that keeps my blood flowing." Then it struck her that he was the angry caller from yesterday afternoon, the man she'd seen peering inside her office door.

"Well, it's damn sure not a heart!"

At that moment Lana Harris appeared outside her back door. "Blair, why is Duchess barking?" She walked onto her lawn and her eyes suddenly brightened in astonishment. "Mitch! Is that you!" she exclaimed, looking with disbelief at the man on Blair's patio.

The Mr. Hyde expression on his face changed abruptly into a smiling Dr. Jekyll. He smiled at Lana as she hurried over, a warm and friendly welcoming smile. "Hey, Lana. How are you? How's Ron?"

Blair watched the exchange with open-mouthed disbelief.

"Oh, he's fine. He's on the golf course"—she twisted her lips—"as usual on Saturday morning. When did you get back?"

"Yesterday afternoon. I caught a flight out of Washington about noon." He glanced at his watch. "I've been in town almost twenty-four hours—and it's incredible what's happened. All thanks to Charlotte and your neighbor here."

Blair jerked up even straighter and her mind clicked away. She couldn't recall anyone in her files named Mitch, or probably Mitchell. But there had definitely been a Charlotte.

"That's not you and Charlotte in the divorce column, is it, Mitch?" Lana asked with a tinge of remorse.

Mitch stood silent for a minute, then said, "'Fraid so."

Blair's eyes rolled upward, as though she had been stricken with the beginning of a seizure. *Oh, my God!* she thought. *Charlotte Morgan.* That case she had questioned so many times in the beginning because the circumstances were so out of the ordinary—the Quit Claim Deed to the property, a settlement so large *and* uncontested. And not a word in response from the husband, William M. Morgan, Jr. William Mitchell Morgan, Jr. Charlotte had called him Bill. Something was screwy. Oh . . . oh . . . oh . . . something was real screwy.

Her mouth fell open and she looked at him again. He stood, still chatting casually with her neighbor.

Then his next comment infuriated her to the depths of her soul.

"When did this shyster move in next to you and Ron?" he asked suddenly, giving a disgusted nod toward Blair.

"Oh," Lana laughed good-naturedly, "Blair's been our neighbor for almost a year now."

"Great. We should all have a good time together. Tell Ron I'll see him later. Maybe we can get out on the links tomorrow. I've decided to stay in town until I get my house back."

"Ron will be delighted," Lana replied enthusiastically, then in a voice heavy with sympathy called to Duchess, "Come on, girl, come on home and let me put some ice on your nose. Come on."

Turning to Blair, he said under his breath, "I'm sure you won't mind a house guest for a few days, will you?"

CHAPTER TWO

Blair watched open-mouthed, speechless, as Lana and the dog left her patio. Then she turned sharply to the man called Mitch, who stood leaning against a corner post of her patio, eyeing her with the most intolerable expression she had ever seen in anyone's eyes. "I don't know what you've got on your mind, Mr. Morgan," she said, fighting back a growing alarm, "but I can tell you here and now you're not stepping one foot inside my home! As a matter of fact, I am now going to have you forceably removed from my property."

Without a single word he strode across the floor, slid back the glass door, and walked casually into the house, broad shoulders swaying with confidence as he passed her.

She rushed in after him. "You get out of my house! Get out or I will most certainly call the police this very moment!"

He shrugged. "Like I said, go ahead." He cut blue glints accusingly at her. "I'd love for the press to get ahold of what you've done! What you did while I was out of the country, thousands of miles from here, working to aid the progress of peace in the world. And now I return to my cozy little home and what have I found? I no longer have a cozy little home. I would love for everyone to know exactly what you've done. Go ahead and call them all! Maybe I can gain enough fame to be invited to the Today show or Phil Donahue. Who knows the potential of this story. It's vast, it's endless, it's overwhelming!"

She roused to battle pitch. "What I did, Mr. Morgan, was follow the letter of the law. I have done nothing illegal. Or immoral. I merely presented a case of evidence before the court and the court moved on the evidence presented. Now, if you have a gripe, you go move in with the judge!"

"No, thank you," he returned with lightning speed. "Judge Walker is old and fat and not at all my type. But you, you're young and beautiful. You may be just what I need to soothe the terrible injustice I've suffered." He stood silently for a moment, eyeing her. "Yes," he said softly, too softly. "I think you might do very well." With deliberate steps he moved toward the front door of the living room. Unlocking the door, he opened it and, standing midway, began hauling his luggage inside—two large bags.

Dumbfounded, Blair watched, shaking her head with disbelief.

He aimed mocking forlorn eyes at her as he placed the second suitcase on her sculptured baby blue carpet. "I had the taxi driver leave my luggage on your porch. I used to have a nice little Jaguar that I used for transportation purposes, but I discovered that Charlotte has that too, through fraud. That's the key word, darling, keep it in mind. Fraud."

"Look, Mr. Morgan, allow me to explain!" she beseeched in a near scream. "I haven't done anything to you! Not a damned thing!" Green eyes flashed. "But I am going to—right now!" She reached for the phone and her fingers curled around the receiver. "You have one minute to remove yourself and your possessions from my house!" She looked at her watch and repeated, "One minute."

"Are you threatening me?" he asked bluntly.

"*You!*" she screamed. "Am I threatening *you*! Am I standing in *your* house! Am I trespassing on *your* property!"

He stood silent a moment. "Okay," he said, "you aren't threatening me. I forgive you."

Her eyes blared. "You forgive me! No wonder your wife divorced you; you're obviously crazy!"

His lips curled upward and he took a step toward her. "That's it. The strain has been too much on me." He spoke softly. "My nervous system has collapsed. My loving wife has left me and taken with her my home, my car, most of my money." He advanced closer. "And when I called her, you know what she said?"

Blair backed away from him cautiously, her eyes wide, her hand still grasping the receiver.

He continued. "She said, 'You will have to take it up with my attorney.' So, darling attorney, here I am to take it up with you. Now, you may call the law if you want, because at this point I am past caring. I would just as soon be in a jail cell as in a hotel room. And as to the charge of being crazy, I assure you my craziest moment occurred at my wedding when I said 'I do' instead of 'shoot me.' "

She couldn't help herself; the expression on his face, the tone of his voice, made her smile—fleetingly. She looked at the phone, gripped by indecision. Finally she moved her hand from it. "All right, Mr. Morgan, I'm not going to call the law at this time, but you *cannot* stay here," she said emphatically. "I'll call you a taxi and you can go back to the hotel."

He sighed. "Well, you might as well call the law, because I am not taking another taxi ride to a hotel. The choice is yours. I'll either stay here or in jail, but I will not spend another night in a hotel. And that's my final word."

She stared gropingly at him. "Uh—listen, don't you have family here?"

His blue eyes grew very round. "Yes. One ex-wife, if you want to call her family. But the more appropriate word would be *thief,* or, better yet, *criminal.* She *has* committed a crime—with your help."

Blair threw up both hands. "I don't want to discuss the case. If you're going to do that, then I'm not talking any further with you."

"Tell you what," he said in a normal tone, "I'll compromise. Monday I'll look for an apartment."

"Why not today!"

"I'm just too tired," he replied very soft. "I've flown thousands of miles. I haven't had any sleep."

"Okay . . . okay, you can use the spare bedroom until Monday. But on Monday, out you go! Understand?"

23

He lifted his bags. "Where might I find this spare bedroom?"

"First door on the left," she replied.

A moment later he called down the hall, "I've always wanted to live in a pink room. It's so lovable and cozy."

She clutched the sides of her head with both hands. How could this be happening! In America! In Virginia! To her! Her wildest imagination wasn't wild enough to envision this predicament for anyone. How could she believe it was actually happening to her? Staring at the carpet, she merely shook her head.

Suddenly she felt his eyes on her and looked around to see him standing in the doorway. "Do you mind if I fix myself some breakfast? I haven't had much of an appetite since I landed yesterday." As he spoke, his clear bright eyes moved down to the top of her strapless one-piece suit and lingered on the boldly exposed flesh of her upper breasts. He smiled with delight.

An involuntary blush came over her face and she yanked fiercely at the top, pulling it up as high as it would go. She gave him a wide-eyed, threatening glare. "You may sleep in my spare bed, use my kitchen, but don't get any ideas that I go with either one. So keep your eyes off my body," she concluded in a clear, distinct tone.

He smiled and winked at her. "Don't worry, darling, I have serious doubts that I could find the woman who took away all my worldly possessions very appealing to me. You're as safe as if you had a large wart on the end of your nose the size of that dog's next door." Chuckling to himself, he turned and retreated to the kitchen.

She knew she had made a serious blunder letting him stay, yet she scarcely wanted to admit it, even to herself. She was amazed with herself, not understanding her own reasoning. Her shoulders slumped a bit as she listened to the opening and closing of cabinets, the clanging of pots and pans.

A moment later she heard the butter melting over the gas burner, sizzling invitingly. Bolting up from the plush white sofa, she bounded into the kitchen, where she placed her hands on her hips. "You do realize, don't you, Mr. Morgan," she said firmly, "that a lawyer must rely on a client's truthfulness and honesty? We don't have the time or resources to investigate each client who comes to us!"

Holding the handle of the iron skillet, he glanced around. "Blair, dear," he said mockingly soft, "I thought we weren't going to discuss the case. Now, be a sweetheart and allow me my eggs without indigestion." A slow grin covered his lips. "Want some?"

"No!"

"It's a cheese omelet. You sure?" The grin deepened and became one-sided as he peered at her from the corners of his eyes.

"No!" she snapped. Looking at the counter and the empty egg carton, she exclaimed, "Did you use *all* those eggs!"

He shrugged innocently. "It wasn't a full dozen," he commented.

Her mouth parted, then she raged, "Almost! It was at least nine, maybe ten!"

Turning full around, he looked emotionlessly at her. "Are you begrudging me a few chicken eggs? Me, the golden goose who laid Charlotte's golden egg?"

In that moment she really looked at him. For the first time she stared moodily into blue eyes the shade of the pale morning sky. His crisp hair was coal black, with a few platinum strands contained in a streak at the right side of his hair line. His nose was long and straight; he had a wide mouth with mockingly full lips covering strong white teeth and a firm jaw with a round, molded chin. In sharp contrast to the pale blue eyes was the sun-darkened skin of his face and neck. She gave one intent sweeping gaze of the lean body confronting her.

Suddenly she spun around and left the kitchen without another hint of a word escaping her lips.

"Where are you going?" he called after her.

She did not reply.

In the hallway her hand went to her brow as she felt her inner calm swiftly deserting her. Why hadn't she evicted this man from her property and placed him under a peace bond to prevent his return? That's what any sane, reasonable person would have done. Did she fear the publicity? This entire situation would definitely bring unwelcomed and unwanted publicity, and could result in her becoming the laughingstock of her profession. Damn it, she had worked too long and too hard to become the punch line of a joke!

Sighing heavily, she went into her bedroom and closed the door softly behind her. She could tolerate this arrangement until Monday; she was certainly

26

that strong. Still, she wished he was ugly, unattractive, with some gross feature like the hunchback of Notre Dame. It wasn't that she hadn't loved poor Quasimodo; it had just taken longer to love him than James Bond.

She grimaced and moved to the closet, thinking that a divorce was supposed to change the life pattern of that particular couple, not the attorney. Changing into something less revealing, green cotton pants and a white blouse complete with collar and short sleeves, she walked over to her desk and lifted a folder from the top drawer. Slowly she pulled out the chair and sat down, staring solemn-eyed through the window above the desk. She hadn't planned to work today, but perhaps a little mental activity would serve to clear her muddled mind.

Looking down at the papers on the desktop, her mind began to travel backward to months before. She recalled the details of the Morgan divorce. Charlotte Morgan had been so convincing, had produced a notarized and recorded quit claim deed to the home. There had been the transfer of title on the Jaguar, also duly processed and registered. Desertion. The plea to the court had been based upon the fact of Charlotte's claim that her husband, William, had deserted her a year ago, that he had run off to parts unknown with his secretary, a woman named Marsha—uh—Marsha something or other, that he had willingly transferred his name from all joint properties to her, Charlotte.

Blair clutched her brow. Damn it! What was that secretary's name, the other woman in the case? Charlotte had sworn under oath that her husband had left in the company of another woman, and that she, his wife, had not heard or been contacted by him in over a year. Of course the divorce had been granted.

And now that husband was in her house, in her kitchen, cooking all her eggs, declaring that he had left, not only the city, but the country, for Uncle Sam. Obviously one or perhaps both of the newly divorced Morgans was lying.

Thoughts became a panic of speculation, but emerged from that state with no clear-cut answers. Acutely aware of the fact that she, as the plaintiff's attorney, had participated in presenting the evidence to the court, she nevertheless knew she could not be held responsible for the outcome. She had merely done what any attorney does—act on behalf of the client. Still, in this particular case she found herself holding the old proverbial bag. Only one word emerged clear when her lips finally moved. "Damn."

For an hour or longer she sat at the bedroom desk, quiet, gloomy-faced, wondering how she had become so thoroughly involved in someone else's problems. Sitting there in the warm spring sunlight, she could look out the window and see the results of marriage; see the children across the street playing in the yard of a neat, well-constructed brick home basically built on the same floor plan as her own, with only the front of the house altered in some aspect.

Absorbed in thought, she watched the neighbor directly across washing his Toyota station wagon, as he did each Saturday morning. Her home was right in the middle of a storybook marriage heaven—an upper middle-class subdivision. But there had been noplace else to buy a home; there were no subdivisions for singles.

As she watched the children playing on the lawn across from her, she straightened, suddenly aware of a complication in her newest plight. Wayne. What would she do with Mitchell Morgan when Wayne arrived to pick her up tonight? How understanding would he be when she would say, "Wayne, I would like you to meet Mitchell Morgan, former husband of one of my clients"? After a moment of intense theorizing about Wayne's reaction, she realized she had no idea what it would be. Although she had known Wayne Fairfield for almost a year, she became aware of how little she did know him. His reaction could run the gamut, from laughter to having a stroke, or anything in between.

Placing her hand over her mouth, she wondered if she should call Wayne and break the dinner engagement. No. No, she would not alter her life-style one iota because of William Mitchell Morgan. Leaning her chin on her cupped hand, she sat for a while longer, wondering about Wayne.

A soft knock sounded at the door and she turned around. "What is it?" she asked loudly.

The door opened and Mitch peered in. Before he spoke, his eyes scanned the room, then jumped from wall to wall, stopping and noticing every picture. "Did you do those?" he asked, eyeing the framed cross-stitched designs on the wall above the queen-size bed.

"No," she replied coolly. "They were gifts."

"Probably from a happy client, no doubt," he said lightly, but with a tinge of sarcasm.

She sat silent, not about to give him the satisfaction of knowing he was right. The two cross-stitched pictures of doves were indeed a gift from a young woman who had gained her freedom from a sadistic brute last year.

Then he transferred his attention down to the bed, the ivory satin spread. His eyes twinkled. "Injustice is everywhere. Here you are with this huge bed and I'm cramped across the hall in an extra-small twin with hardly enough—"

"Hotels have large beds, Mr. Morgan."

His eyes fastened on hers. "I know," he sighed. "But for some reason I'd rather be here." Slowly his gaze went to the table beside her bed, staring at a half-eaten apple and an open pack of peanuts. He turned an amused smile back to her. "Oh, no, you're a muncher."

Feeling flushed, she replied quickly, avoiding his eyes. "What I am is of no concern to you. Now, would you please remove yourself from my bedroom."

Not in the least disturbed by her request, he complained good-naturedly, "I can't find a dishtowel. I looked everywhere in the kitchen, in all the cabinet drawers, under the sink, then I figured you must be one of those people who put things where they don't belong."

Pursing her lips, she did not reply immediately, then she coolly said, "The dishtowels are in the linen closet. The linen closet is the next door from where you are standing. Do not use the new ones."

He laughed and started toward her.

"Stop right there, turn around, and get out of my bedroom."

His eyes, still full of amusement, met hers. "I worry about your bedside manner."

"You have me confused with a doctor. I don't have a bedside manner."

"You aren't very understanding, at any rate," he pointed out. "Have you considered how I felt when I stepped off the plane yesterday and found my home, not invaded, but gone? My car, the bank account, the savings, gone. Lucky for me I did my banking in Switzerland while I was in the Mideast." His eyes darkened as he touched his lips thoughtfully. "Tell me, why didn't you and Charlotte try to take control of my company? Wasn't it impressive enough?"

Blair's eyes widened. "What company?"

"My company, Morgan Sheetrock, Incorporated. Didn't Charlotte tell you that I also had a company?"

She shook her head. "No, there was no mention of a company. None at all."

Drawing his lips into a tight straight line, he looked at her a long moment before relaxing his mouth to say, "You see what a smart woman you represented. Charlotte knew that if she involved my company in the divorce the fact would be discovered that I had not deserted her, but had accepted a government contract to teach the Saudi the art of manufacturing and hanging sheetrock," he declared bitterly.

"I'm sorry, Mitch." Her voice once again precise was charged with emotion. "I had no idea. I know you think I'm responsible, but I'm not. If you think you're a victim, is it not possible that I am also a victim?"

Rubbing one finger thoughtfully at the bridge of his perfectly shaped nose, he kept his eyes on her. "I have never heard of anything like this happening to a man before. I just, for the love of God, cannot figure out how you two did this."

She leaned forward in the chair toward him. "I followed the law. I did what I do in all my cases like yours. I placed a notice in the paper for the time specified by law. Why didn't some of your friends or relatives come forward? Why wasn't I informed by someone?"

He considered the question as his eyes lowered. When he finally looked up, he said, "I suppose because no one knew that those notices you placed in the paper pertained to me. No one knows me as William. And by the fact my company wasn't mentioned, no one knew."

Blair deliberately rose and faced him. "What about the woman named Marsha?"

With wide-eyed disbelief, he glared at her. "Marsha?" he breathed in unmasked surprise.

"Yes." Blair stepped toward him slowly. "The petition for divorce states that you deserted your wife for a woman named Marsha—something. I've forgotten her last name."

"Partlow," he volunteered quickly with raised brows. "Marsha Partlow."

Blair nodded. "Yes. That's the name. Did you?"

Refusing to answer, he spun around and walked

back to the door. "Linen closet, next door to the right," he said, moving from the room.

Not answering, she stood watching the door long after it had closed behind him. With a sigh she went back and resumed her seat at the desk. The first skill to learn was the art of considering all possibilities for cause. There were so many possibilities in this case, it boggled her mind. Both parties could be lying. Both could be telling the truth, or at least a partial truth. One could be telling the truth, one could be lying. Both could be telling partial lies. The possibilities were endless. But one thing for sure—she had been caught up in the middle of this terrible mess, and she intended to find out the truth. At that moment it ranked high beside the most earnest desire she had ever known.

Her eyes fastened on the half-eaten darkened apple on the bedside table, and a strained expression covered her face. She shook her head quickly and heaved a deep sigh. No, absolutely not! She didn't care how handsome he was. She didn't care if both his feet and head hung over the ends of the twin bed. She absolutely would not entertain thoughts of making his stay more comfortable.

She swore she would spend the remainder of the day avoiding him. She stayed in her room until lunch, then traveled by herself to a nearby Burger King for a hamburger, and afterward spent an hour or so shopping, making the grocery store her last stop before returning to the house at a still early hour.

When she drove her Buick Skylark into the drive and turned off the engine, the front door opened and he stepped outside onto the small concrete porch. Placing his hand on one small pillar, he leaned toward her and called out, "Anything I can help you with?"

Briefly she was tempted to say no, but instead called back, "You can bring in the groceries."

Insensible as it seemed to be, she had not been disappointed to see him stroll out onto her porch. He had changed clothes and was dressed in tan casual slacks and matching shirt, his face freshly shaven, his dark hair tousled from towel drying.

He approached the car with a smile, which she ignored, reaching at once to open the rear door, then holding it open for him to get the groceries from the back seat. Seeing his lean body bent over, she gave a second sweeping glance at him and decided this would never do for any length of time. It would be too easy to like his looks.

"I thought we might go out to dinner tonight," he said politely, moving forward, holding the two bags of groceries in his arms, peering at her around one. "I haven't eaten in an American restaurant in thirteen and a half months."

Moving forward in step beside him, she replied, "I already have an engagement tonight. But thank you." The fragrant scent of his fresh aftershave filling the air about them, she looked up at the dusky sky, though watching him covertly from the corners of her eyes.

His mouth twitched slightly. "With Wayne?" he asked unsmiling.

Catching her breath, she exclaimed, "How did you know?"

34

Walking into the house, he looked over his shoulder at her as she stood holding the door for him. "Two ways—the cards in your kitchen drawer and he called about thirty minutes ago."

"How dare you read my cards!" she said sharply.

"I couldn't help myself. I saw them when I was looking for the dishtowel. They were just lying there asking to be read. 'Blair, when the roses you see, think of me. All my love, Wayne.' And 'Blair, a golden chain for the girl who holds my heart captive. Always, Wayne.' And the one I really liked—"

"That's quite enough, Mr. Morgan," she flared angrily, her eyes blurring with fury. "In case you don't know, it's terribly rude to read someone's personal mail." She wanted to bop the back of his perfectly shaped head as she followed him into the kitchen. "And just what did you say to him when he called?" she asked icily.

He placed the groceries on the table, then turned and grinned at her. "I said you were gone. I didn't know where, or when you would be back, or even *if* you would be back. After all, you did leave without giving me your itinerary."

There was no hesitation in her cool comeback. "Well, I'm sure he'll call again."

His grin spread. "And what if he doesn't?" he asked lightly, arching dark brows at her.

"He will," she returned with much self-assurance. After giving him a go-to-hell look, she began to put away the groceries.

"Would you like me to help you?" he offered with a generous smile.

"No, I wouldn't," she replied curtly. "The best

35

help you can be is to take yourself somewhere and sit down, preferably in another room." With narrowed eyes she stacked cans on the cabinet shelf.

He seated himself at the table and stretched long legs in front of him, his heels resting in the middle of the floor. "How long have you been an attorney?"

"Long enough to know what you're doing is illegal," she shot back over her shoulder.

With a devilish glint he said, "Ah, but not long enough apparently to know what you did is also illegal." He laughed, then asked teasingly, "Tell me, did you pass your bar exam the first time?"

"I certainly did," she replied shortly. She turned her head and glared at him. "Does that surprise you?"

He chuckled. "That word has been eliminated from my vocabulary. Nothing surprises me, and I do mean nothing. When you've had the ultimate surprise, the word loses its meaning."

Brushing her hands on the back of her pants, she turned to face him, and for a moment their eyes locked before she looked away. He was certainly easy to look at, astonishingly easy.

Staring idly out the window at the gathering layer of low gray clouds, she asked, "It didn't rain much where you were, did it?"

"Much?" he repeated lightly. "Not much, not at all. The only clouds I saw were golden sand clouds. But those people over there don't miss the rain. You don't miss what you've never known." His strong jaw firmed and his lips tightened in a line, then relaxed, saying, "I can't count the mornings I walked outside, looked around, and said to myself, 'All the oil in the world can't buy a mountain from those magnificent Shenandoahs.' " He paused. "Tell me, have you traveled much?"

"Just here in this country. We took long summer vacations when I was growing up. My parents both taught school, so they were keen on their children knowing the history of this country. All our vacations were learning ones, but still exciting."

"Do you have the desire to travel abroad?"

She gave a little shake of her head. "Not extensively. There are some places I would like to see—London, Paris, Rome, Athens." Suddenly she laughed, adding, "Switzerland, Africa, Australia . . ."

"But not extensively," he joked, "just a quick little jaunt to every country."

She held up one finger and chuckled. "But I didn't say Siberia or the two poles; *that* would make it extensive." For a moment she stood mesmerized by his smiling face. Then slowly the smile faded from her own lips. She was talking and laughing with him as if she had known him all her life, not at all like someone she had met only hours earlier.

Self-consciously she cast her eyes down. "Well, I have things to do," she offered in a low voice, taking herself in a path around him toward the door.

His gaze followed her. "Are you sure of your date for the evening?"

Her composure regained, she said confidently, "As sure as rain."

CHAPTER THREE

The beautiful bright spring morning faded into an overcast afternoon and stormy black night. The soft rumbling of thunder could be heard in a continuous roll with occasional flashes of lightning. Blair and Wayne Fairfield were in his car on the way to dinner when he looked over to her and said, "Looks like rain."

She turned her eyes from the window and smiled at him. Wayne, the owner of a jewelry store, was something more than the fakes on his bargain table and something less than the brilliant diamonds in his display case. An even-tempered young man, Blair had yet to see him emotional over anything—even her. Of medium height, fair-haired, and fair skinned, he was striking and neat, but not handsome. Not in the sense of the handsome pouting face she had left in her kitchen minutes earlier when she dashed out the front door without inviting Wayne inside.

She studied the driver of the car through narrowed eyes fringed with long dark lashes. Her date for the evening was a perfect gentleman, completely bypassed by the sexual revolution. He opened doors, pulled out chairs, displayed unusual attentiveness, and his hands never strayed beyond her shoulders. He was a pleasant change; he was different, but at times boring beyond belief.

The relationship had become one of those patterns of life established before consciously realizing one had been. Saturday evening dinner, or a movie, or both. Blair had wanted to break it off for several weeks now, but somehow couldn't work up the courage to say the words for fear of hurting his feelings, for fear he wouldn't understand.

In spite of the growing number of divorces, acceptable male escorts in this city numbered far less than females. There seemed to be an adequate supply under the age of twenty-five, or over the age of fifty, but neither age group interested her. At twenty-nine she preferred someone in her own age range, and that's what she had with Wayne, who was thirty-two. But with a low sigh she realized that that was all she had—someone in her own age range.

They had almost reached the restaurant when he said without looking at her, "Blair, I wouldn't want you to think I'm prying, but who was that man who answered your phone this afternoon?"

Feeling the rush of color to her cheeks, she gave her head several quick little shakes and said, "Oh, no one you would know, Wayne."

"I know that," he answered blankly. "But that doesn't tell me who he is."

She blinked, groping for an answer, much too embarrassed to tell the truth of his identity. Finally one last shake of her head and the words scrambled out. "He's—uh—Daddy's younger brother." She closed her mouth tightly, feeling absolutely foolish for telling such a lie.

Wayne didn't say anything for a minute, then said abruptly, "I didn't know your dad had a younger brother. I thought you had only the one aunt in Washington, D. C."

A second passed and she declared in a low voice, with an uneasy laugh, "That's because he's adopted." She was ready for the discussion to end. But, much to her dismay, Wayne seemed fascinated.

"Really." He sounded astonished. "That's very interesting, Blair. He didn't sound like an elderly man."

"Well, he's much older than he sounds," she said quickly, then added, "or looks." She felt like the fly caught in her own web of lies.

Wayne nodded thoughtfully. "I'd like to meet him when we get back to your house. You know, I've never met any of your family." Suddenly he laughed. "This is great . . . your uncle." He nodded again. "Yep, it's great. What does he do?"

Her heart began to slow as she struggled to support the original lie. "He's unemployed at present. That's why he's visiting. He thought he would see all the relatives while he's between jobs."

Wayne whipped the car into the lighted parking lot beside the building housing the restaurant. When he turned off the motor he continued with the questioning. "What's his name?"

"Mitch . . . Mitchell Morgan," she answered, then bit her tongue.

He looked over at her once more before reaching for the door. "Not Bennett? Didn't he take the Bennett name when he was adopted?"

His door opened and she had until he walked around to her side to come up with another lie. His brows were raised waiting for the answer when her door opened.

She smiled sweetly and slid out. When she straightened, she said, "Yes, his name is Mitchell Morgan Bennett." She had done it finally. His curiosity was satisfied.

After a quiet meal, during which he asked a half-dozen times if she wasn't hungry tonight, they returned to the car in silence.

On the way home at ten o'clock, she rolled her eyes frantically. She had tried to talk Wayne into a late movie, but he was much to enthused about meeting a member of her "family."

"He may already be in bed, Wayne," she pointed out with frustration. "He was awfully tired when I left."

Wayne gave a nod of his head in understanding. "If he is, we won't disturb him, but it's not yet ten, so maybe he's still up."

The side of her mouth facing away from him curled up in utter dismay. Wayne had not been this excited about anything since the movie *E. T.* It was a curious sensation to know she was about to be caught in the biggest lie of her life. The best she could hope for would be that they would find the house darkened and quiet.

When they drove up in the drive she saw the house lit up like a Christmas tree. Even the porch light was on, along with the outside floodlights. If the sky had not been so dark and stormy, it would have looked like day.

Her shoulders sagged a bit as Wayne laughed low with obvious delight. "I don't think he's in bed, Blair."

She laughed weakly. "That doesn't necessarily mean anything, Wayne. He's always been afraid of storms. He sleeps with all the lights on, always has." The lies were coming easier. She hardly had to think about that one.

But when they stepped onto the porch and heard the television, she knew she had been caught. She paused at the door and looked directly at Wayne's expectant face. "Why don't I plan to prepare dinner for us all Monday night, Wayne. If I did that, you could get on back home before the storm hits."

Much to her dismay, before Wayne could reply, the front door opened. She looked around to see Mitch Morgan standing there in pajamas and robe, peering directly at her. "There's a storm coming," he said. "Don't you two want to come inside before you get struck by lightning?" Then he shrugged and stepped out of the door, holding it open wide for them to enter.

With a wince on her face she walked in, Wayne close on her heels. For a moment she stood absolutely motionless and speechless.

Then Wayne stepped forward, extending his hand to Mitch. "I'm Wayne Fairfield, Mr. Bennett."

She watched Mitch's head cock to one side in

puzzlement, then Wayne went on with, "It's a real pleasure to finally meet a member of Blair's family."

Mitch looked first to Blair, one brow raised. Then a slow, almost sinister grin spread across his lips. Her blue-green irises fastened hard on him, daring him to give her away.

Smoothly he turned to Wayne, grasping the hand that had been in the air for a long moment and shook it with an overabundance of feeling. Chuckling, he said, "It's been a long time since anyone called me Mr. Bennett. Just call me Mitch, why don't you." Releasing the grasp on Wayne's hand, his arm reached out and he pulled Blair hard to his side in a tight squeeze. "Of all my relatives Blair is my favorite." His fingers pinched into her waist, pulling her closer against his firm, lean side.

A fluttering sensation caught in the pit of her stomach and she freed herself from him with staggering quickness. "*Uncle* Mitch," she said with much emphasis. "I know how tired you are, so please don't let us keep you from bed." She leveled the most inconspicuous threatening stare she could manage with Wayne watching her.

"I know"—he took a deep breath—"that you two young lovers want to be alone, so this old uncle will leave you." He sighed. "I suppose we can take up those pressing family matters in the morning." He shook Wayne's hand once more. "Good night, Wayne." He paused and looked at Blair. "Good night, sweet niece," he murmured, and bent his face to hers.

She saw his lips coming in a fast direct path to hers and her head jerked back so abruptly it almost gave her whiplash. She turned her face so that his mouth caught her cheek. Stepping back, she gave him a dimpled smirk and a throaty, "'Night."

He turned, walked across the living room, and went down the hall whistling, "Hello, Young Lovers," which finally became muffled behind the closed bedroom door.

Catching her lower lip between her teeth, she turned to Wayne, who was looking at her questioningly. "Blair, you don't seem to be very fond of him," he finally said.

Releasing her lip, she stated matter-of-factly, "No one in the family is, Wayne. We just put up with him because we don't know what else to do." She was glad she wasn't Pinocchio or her nose would have extended past the front porch by now. But she acknowledged the fact that the lies had worked and that was much better than having the truth known about this arrangement.

Wayne looked troubled. "That's too bad," he muttered worriedly. "He seemed like an all right guy." His brow wrinkled. "But much younger than I expected. He doesn't look much older than me."

"Wayne," she said harshly, "let's not discuss him anymore. I told you he didn't look his age."

"Well, how old is he?" Wayne threw back. "He certainly doesn't look over thirty-five."

Her brows raised. "Didn't you see that gray streak; he's pushing fifty."

"Damn," Wayne grunted. "I want his secret."

She sighed impatiently. She had intended to keep Wayne with her until Mitch was in a sound sleep, but it wasn't worth it. "I've enjoyed the evening, Wayne,

44

but if you don't mind, I think I'll turn in myself. The week has really taken a lot out of me."

He nodded with understanding. "I saw the fruits of your labor in the morning paper. It's tragic, isn't it?"

She breathed aloud. "You'll never know just how tragic."

After Wayne had gone, she stood, then swayed against the closed door. She listened, and when his car pulled away she began to flip light switches off. She had never been in such a strained predicament. She was actually fearful to go down the hall to her own bedroom.

Falling onto the sofa, she kicked off her shoes and curled her feet up under her. Outside, the storm grew nearer, the thunder louder, the lightning flashing more and more frequently. She clasped her hands together and lay her head back. The way her luck was running, she would probably get blown away with Mitch Morgan in her house, and her reputation would be ruined in spite of all her efforts.

She crossed her arms across her chest and hugged herself tightly, trying to control her apprehension. Suddenly she heard his steps in the hallway, then a second later in the kitchen. The faucet came on and she heard a steady stream of water filling a container. Having him in the house was definitely not the uncomplicated situation she had believed it would be. She was acutely aware of him and with each passing second the awareness grew.

"I'm making a pot of coffee," he called out. "We can sit in here until the storm passes. Why don't you go get comfortable; it may be a long night."

The sound of his voice brought a flurry of mixed emotions. "Sounds good," she called out, but remained unmoving a few minutes, then rose from the sofa and went slowly down the hall to her bedroom, changing into the slacks and shirt she had worn earlier in the day.

With faltering steps she entered the kitchen. The coffee was in cups on the table. Obviously comfortable in his pajamas and robe, Mitch sat a bit slumped in a chair, his long legs stretched and crossed at the ankles. "Smells good." She smiled faintly, pulling out a chair at the far end of the table from him and bringing her cup from where he had placed it next to his.

After stirring in a spoonful of sugar, her eyes flickered to his face, then away. He was staring at the floor, his lean face thoughtful, his attention seemingly somewhere beyond the kitchen, maybe even beyond the storm outside. "Mitch," she began hesitantly, opening the conversation, "you know that I'm bound by ethics that prevent me from divulging information given to me by your former wife, but if you should want to discuss what's happened over this cup of coffee, I will listen."

His shoulders straightened back against the chair and he sighed heavily, then shrugged. "What would it accomplish?" he asked pensively.

She pressed on. "I would like to understand. I really would."

"Understand?" Unexpectedly he laughed, a sound remarkably close to bitterness. "In order for you to understand, Blair, I would have to tell you about Charlotte, and for some reason I'm not exactly up to discussing her. One storm a night is enough, don't you think?"

"What do you plan to do?" Blair asked softly.

"I plan to get it all back," he stated without hesitation, glancing around at her. "You see, what's been done is not only highly improper, but also illegal." He shook his head. "I don't know why she's done this, for what purpose." His eyes narrowed. "Even a woman scorned doesn't usually go to these extremes."

Blair's eyes rounded. "Was she scorned?"

His tongue traveled slowly around his teeth. "Three years ago I asked Charlotte for a divorce. It was then I realized we didn't have anything to build on. Our marriage had become like bad sheetrock, brittle and crumbling. It was at that time I accepted my first contract for work outside the country. I was gone a year and I hoped when I returned that some things would have changed in the marriage." A puzzled expression caught his features, a near pain filled his eyes. "We had our disappointments, as every couple does, but nothing we shouldn't have coped with. Who knows what changes people, what makes a perfectly lovely person become a devious schemer who will do anything to get what she wants." He raised his brows skeptically and repeated in a whisper, "Who knows?" He emptied his cup, rose from his chair, and poured more coffee. Looking at her cup and finding it half empty, he warmed it, then walked back and eased the coffeepot onto the counter. With a faint smile on his lips, he said, "Have you ever been married?"

"No," came the hasty reply and soft laugh. "And

47

from all I've seen and heard, the case against is presently much stronger than the one for."

He seated himself again and peered at her through half-closed lids. "You're very pretty." A hint of a smile played on his lips. "I like the way your hair curls around your face. You have very pretty hair."

She stirred uncomfortably in her chair. "I imagine any woman would look pretty to you after thirteen months in a highly restrictive country."

He chuckled. "How correct you are. Some types of behavior is simply not allowed. But, as busy as we were, we hardly had time to notice." He paused for a moment, then added, "Tonight, I've noticed."

Her gaze fell to the tabletop as his words echoed around the room. She could feel his unwavering eyes fastened on her lowered head, daring her to look up.

Suddenly she thought of the woman who had traveled out of the country with him, and there came a sudden pang of anxiety to know about her. How did she fit into this awful situation?

The silence in the room became extended. Outside, the storm was raging; a loud rumbling could be heard overhead, with a continuous bright flash of light flickering across the dark sky. The rain beat down in a new birth of fierceness.

Raising her head, she stated with a low sigh, "Sounds like the storm is going all out tonight."

His eyes burned into hers and she read his thoughts. His stare hypnotized her, a long steady look with glints of fire vivid in the blueness.

"Blair," he whispered, "you don't realize how great you look, how—"

"No, Mitch, don't do that," she interrupted, a

tightness in her chest binding her words. "I don't want to realize," she said quickly, softly.

He looked at his cup of coffee, then up with a smile. "Okay, no problem. If you don't want me to tell you that you're the most delectable dish in this kitchen, I won't."

She made no reply, but did not miss the dancing glint in his blue irises.

He sat studying her more closely. "Why did you go to all the trouble of hiding my true identity from your date? Wouldn't he approve of an overnight guest?"

"I saw no reason to go into an explanation with him," she answered with a shrug.

"So you told a little white lie?" he pursued.

"Yes," she admitted openly. "I did."

The wind picked up, and through the window she could see the tops of the pines bending outside. She sprang from her chair and closed the checkered kitchen curtains tightly. Before she had released the fabric she felt arms come around her middle. She gasped and immediately her fingers clasped his arms hard. "Don't do that," she said firmly, prying at his arms. Still, she was acutely aware his touch aroused a kind of unwelcomed wild excitement in her.

He chuckled and his lips nuzzled into the back of her hair, his breath burning her scalp. "Do what? I'm not doing anything. What am I doing?" he whispered jokingly, his body curved into hers.

Bringing an elbow back, she pushed against his chest. "Mitch—let—me—go!" she exclaimed strongly, realizing her immunity to him was fast leaving.

He seized her tighter, so tight she could not move

her elbows, so tight he was severing her breath. His chin pressed into her shoulder and he whispered close to her ear, "Or what?" he chided. "What will you do if I don't let you go?"

"You will," she answered softly, threateningly. "Because you are too smart not to. Now, let me go this instant or you'll be sorry you ever met me!"

His lips plowed through her hair and he kissed her ear. "How sorry?" he whispered.

She felt her knees going first, melting right out from under her. "Real sorry," she choked in a whisper.

The storm outside was raging, shaking the house. A bright flash of lightning lit the room momentarily as his lips traveled from her ear to her neck and softly pressed into it. Tension sprang up in her body, drawing her mind away from the reality of this incomprehensible situation to the unrealistic yearning of her body. She was very much torn by her reaction to him. A part of her sought release, but the stronger part didn't.

His soft lips touched her neck again and her eyes closed. Her hands clutching his arms firmly began to lose their grip. Her fingers softened. His parted lips playing at her neck sent a warmth creeping from deep within outward like a great spider web of spinning fire.

Slowly he turned her in his arms, drawing her around to kiss one cheek, then the other, before placing his lips lightly on her mouth.

Her hands spread at his shoulders, somewhat reluctantly, to push him away from her. Her eyes opened to find his closed and a feeling of alarm swept through her. What was he doing? No, she knew what he was doing. The real question was what was she doing?

The confusion mounted and she pulled her mouth away from his, opening it wide to voice a loud protest. His hands caught her face at both sides and before she could utter a sound his mouth recaptured hers in a hard, circling kiss, his tongue moving sensually between her teeth in a tantalizing search to meet hers.

Unspoken words swelled in her throat as her tongue withdrew to escape his touch. Her actions did not stop him. Almost fiercely he crushed hard into her mouth, bringing a sudden ache to life down lower along her body. In spite of herself, desire stirred, and so did her senses. She realized how tense she had grown, her insides tightening to a dangerous pitch. She jerked her head quickly, freeing her mouth from his hungry assault. "You—you—" she gasped breathlessly. "You fool!"

He stood open-mouthed, his eyes fixed on her face. Slowly his tongue circled his lips and his arms relaxed, then finally dropped from around her. His breath came in a rush, and when he spoke his words emerged shakily, "I'm sorry—I didn't mean—"

Extremely agitated, she interrupted, "I don't give a damn what you meant, or didn't mean. I told you —hands off!"

With a start he threw out, "Aren't you overreacting to a single kiss, Blair? For God's sake, it was only a kiss."

A loud rumble of thunder shook the walls and at the same time a terrible blinding bolt of lightning flashed inside, lighting the room bone white, then disappearing again into the muted darkness. The rain raged with such a force it sounded as if it would beat through the ceiling.

He stood holding her arm firmly, pale blue eyes searching hers. In that moment she felt very far away from the storm outside. She could hardly hear the downpour for the roaring in her ears. "Please, Mitch," she said much softer. "Let me go."

He moved one step closer and whispered, "What if I can't? What if I can't help myself?" His face was close to hers, so close his warm breath burned her lips.

Quickly her head lowered and she drew back. With her free hand she brushed one side of her hair away from her face. "Don't take your spite out on me; I don't deserve it."

He suddenly released his grip on her arm. "Is that what you think, that this is spite? You think that?"

"What else can I think?" she answered huskily. "Isn't anger your driving force at the moment? Don't you blame me for what's happened to you? Aren't you trying to use my body to seek a release for your frustrations with me? Isn't revenge your greatest and overriding motivation?" Her brows rose. "Isn't it?"

He paused another second, then turned abruptly and muttered, "Ah, hell," under his breath. He re-seated himself at the kitchen table.

He sat wide-eyed and silent as she walked from the kitchen in fast, stiff steps.

Closing the door to her bedroom, she stripped from her clothes in a daze and pulled on her night-gown. Then she spun around and stared blankly at the door, torn over whether or not to turn the lock. She wanted to touch him; she wanted his touch. She had never experienced such inner confusion.

She walked to the door and stretched her hand, then drew it back without touching the lock. Her hand whisked across her face, then caught her lips. It was ridiculous to lock a door in her own house. Did she need the security of a lock to keep him out of her bed? At that moment she was not quite sure, but one thing she knew—doors were too easy to unlock.

CHAPTER FOUR

She got into bed and pulled the sheet high around her neck. Nestled comfortably, she lay motionless, all her senses absorbed in sounds. The rain still pattered lightly on the roof along with the sound of Mitch moving around in the kitchen, water running in the sink. She realized he was washing the coffeepot and cups. Her breath caught in a curious little gasp and she closed her eyes tightly. The sounds were unusually magnified.

She heard him slide the chairs under the table, heard the soft scrape of wood on the linoleum. There came a silence, then the refrigerator door opened and closed. Her tense body began to relax. If he was getting himself something to eat, it seemed very likely that his thoughts had strayed away from her, at least for the present. She sighed a long breath of relief.

Her body warmed the sheets, and against that

natural warmth she could not help but think of Mitch's dilemma—and wonder. What had happened was neither clear-cut nor easy to understand. There were too many whys. Why would any woman divorce a man such as William Mitchell Morgan? Her gut instinct told her he was indeed the victim. But why? What part did the other woman, Marsha Partlow, play in the overall picture? Why had he deeded the house and transferred the car to Charlotte? And if he had, why the act of surprise now to find his possessions gone? But the biggest why was if Charlotte had obtained the property through fraud —why? What could she possibly hope to gain by such action? The more she thought about it, the more confusing the entire matter became.

Of course her interest was founded on more than idle curiosity. As legal counsel for the plaintiff it was possible she had unknowingly participated in an unethical procedure. She was concerned for herself and her own career as much, or more, than any other factor. Her personal ambition was not so great that she would knowingly or willingly violate the law in order to achieve any measure of success.

She knew in the days to come all the whys would be answered and she could only hope she would emerge unscathed from it all. First thing Monday she would pull the file and begin her own analysis of what had taken place in the civil action of Morgan vs. Morgan.

She lay quiet and still on her side, her legs drawn up, her half-closed eyes looking at the window lighted by the streetlights, watching the moisture gather and run in little trails along the pane. The rain had finally stopped.

She heard a sound and then slowly the door opened. In that moment her heart hesitated, almost stopping.

"Are you asleep, Blair?" Mitch whispered in a low voice.

She did not answer, instead she closed her eyes. She listened to the sound of his steps on the carpet, the rustle of pajama legs as he walked slowly, deliberately, to beside her bed. She wasn't sure she was breathing, but she was sure of the trembling deep inside her.

Eyes closed, she struggled to remain absolutely motionless as though asleep. She heard a sound she could not make out, then felt his shadow fall across her. She waited breathlessly, not daring to open her eyes.

She felt his hand touch her hair lightly, his fingers playing with a single curl. Her heart had begun to beat so thunderingly hard she feared he could hear it.

A brief second passed and his fingers left her hair. She heard steps take him back across the room and the sound of the door closing gently filled her ears. She lay with lids tightly shut for a full minute until she heard the door across the hall close. Trembling all over, she cautiously opened her eyes. There on the table next to the bed was a big round apple. Releasing a long sigh, the corners of her mouth curled and the hint of dimples appeared in both cheeks. She felt strangely victorious. There was no way he could know how close she had come to opening her eyes and looking up at him, how much she had wanted to reach up and take his hand away from her hair and clasp it to her breasts. She had not been exactly face to face with desire, but she had been within a hand's reach—and she had not reached. Even wanting to, she had not. That made her feel good about herself. With a smile on her lips she looked at the apple until she drifted into a calm, peaceful sleep.

She awoke to a bright rain-washed day and the smell of bacon frying filled her nostrils. For a few seconds she could not put her muddled thoughts in order, then she suddenly remembered she was not alone.

She raised herself up and yawned wide, then shook her head. She was sitting there in the middle of her bed when his head poked in the door.

"You know what I want more than anything today, Blair?" he asked abruptly without the pleasantries of any greeting.

"What?" she asked with some suspicion.

He smiled. "To spend the day in the mountains. I thought about it last night. That's why I'm cooking breakfast, so we can get an early start."

Her mouth pursed. "We?" she repeated softly, raising her brows and giving her head a few soft shakes no.

He walked across the room to the window and looked out, then cut his eyes to her. "I think more than anything I missed the mountains, real mountains. I've seen enough barren land and sand dunes to last me a lifetime." Facing her, he walked over slowly and held out his hands. "Ready to get up?"

57

She drew away from his touch and slowly folded her arms around her knees, resting her chin on her kneecaps. "I'm able to get out of bed without assistance," she announced, eyeing him with uncertainty. Her gaze swept his body. He was dressed in form-fitting khakis and a short-sleeve knit shirt that molded to him nicely. Her gaze then moved restlessly past him to the window. Moments like this made her acutely aware of how vulnerable she was to his lean good looks. "There's a weekend craft show in the park," she finally explained. "I had planned on going."

Nodding his head slowly, disappointment covered his face. "I see." Then with a quick shrug he added, "Breakfast is ready anyway." He moved across the room and hesitated at the door, saying, "I like how you look first thing in the morning."

His words jarred her. She had rather he not say nice things to her. When the door closed behind him, she felt a strange agony.

She got out of bed, went into her bathroom, washed her face, and brushed her teeth. Then pulling on a long-sleeve floor-length robe, she tied it securely and walked into the hallway.

When she entered the kitchen, he asked vaguely over his shoulder, "How do you like your eggs?"

"Over well," she answered equally as vaguely.

He stood in silence, frying the eggs.

"What can I do?" she asked, looking around to find everything already done.

He turned slowly, and in a voice hardly audible, yet low and suggestive, he said, "I have a few ideas."

She turned her head aside quickly. "I didn't mean —" she stammered, "I meant . . ."

"I know what you meant," he said, turning off the burners. He paused for a moment, then took a step toward her.

Startled, she moved back from him until she stood in the doorway. "Mitch, I am not going to become involved with you. I'm not!" she said emphatically.

"I envy your strength, Blair," he spoke softly.

She pointed to her own chest, jabbing herself several quick times. "This is me, the woman who helped take away all your worldly possessions. Remember? Only yesterday you declared I was as appealing to you as the dog next door."

Stepping in front of her, he touched her cheek. "That's the way with you attorneys. Look how you twisted my words. What I said was if you had a wart on the end of your nose the size of the dog's next door. But you don't; you have a pert little nose, one that I'm becoming extremely fond of." With one finger he raised her chin and his lips brushed the end of her nose.

His closeness, his lips, perfectly paralyzed her. Her gaze fixed on his, and she looked deeper and deeper into the blueness, so deep she could see the longing, could feel his longing. His eyes were two spreading blue seas pulling her under, catching her first at the knees.

He reached out his arms toward her and like a magnet she found herself drawing into his embrace almost helplessly, as if some incomprehensible force had taken hold of her senses. A low moan escaped his lips when he kissed her mouth slowly, torturingly slowly, bringing to life sensations so intense she felt the overpowering need to defend herself from them.

Stunned, she pushed away from him with such fierceness he gasped with surprise. "Don't do that again," she protested, then quickly lightened her tone and added, "Not before breakfast."

He surveyed her with a glint in his eyes, but said nothing.

After they were seated at the table, he said, "I'd like to come along with you today; that is, if you don't mind." He gave a one-sided grin. "It's been forever since I've seen a craft show."

"Have you ever been to one?"

"No." He grinned. "But I've always wanted to go. That is, if I could go with someone who looks just like you."

She hesitated. "Do you think it's wise, Mitch? A craft show is very public."

He shrugged. "I don't see any reason to hide from the public. I'm not a criminal. Besides, I don't think we'll run into any of my old crowd. Craft shows aren't their style."

"Okay," she said in agreement. "Fine with me, but if later you find yourself sorry that you didn't go to the mountains as you had intended, don't blame me."

He smiled and said softly, "The mountains will always be there."

In spite of the many people crowded into the park, Blair did not see a single person she knew. With Mitch at her side they walked leisurely to all the booths and stands, looking, sometimes examining

60

the various items on display. She glanced often at Mitch, trying to see if he was enjoying himself and was encouraged by his expression of interest.

Midway around the park, he said quietly, "Boy, there's all kind of talent here, isn't there?"

She nodded. "Yes, everything on display is handmade."

"Uhmmm, busy hands." A step later his own right hand slid behind her waist and he whispered, "Inspiring."

Removing his hand, she replied without hesitation, "Don't get too inspired." She gave him a sudden reproachful sweep of the eyes. "*These* hands all worked to make something."

He looked at her with a sudden devilish grin. "Counsellor, as we continue our walk I want you to consider that statement and all its implications." Then he looked innocently over to the next booth, displaying rows of wood-carved figures.

She flushed, but offered no more of her crafty logic.

At noon they ordered a hamburger and coffee at a tent at the far end of the park. Mitch, carrying the food in a cardboard container, came around the table and slid onto the bench across from her. He placed her hamburger and coffee in front of her and passed her one of the napkins. "Be neat," he joked. "The woman at the register would only let me have these two napkins. I picked up several and she slapped my hand and made me put back all but two."

"I saw her." Blair laughed. "I wondered what you'd done." Surprised at her own good mood, she realized how very much she enjoyed having Mitch with her, even though she had periodically told herself how much better off she would be if he weren't. She was beginning to feel very much at ease, comfortable with him. It wasn't ideal in her particular position.

Swallowing a large bite of hamburger, his eyebrows shot up. "I still can't believe the price on those dolls. Two hundred dollars—for a doll!"

She laughed softly. "Those dolls are very popular, Mitch."

"They're plain ugly. Their faces are all pinched up. Do little girls really want dolls like those?"

"Yes. Believe me, little girls like those dolls. You saw how they were selling."

He finished off the hamburger and while chewing stated, "If I had my choice, I'd take a Barbie."

She rolled her eyes up at him. "You would," she stated blandly, then added as an afterthought, "but if you had a little girl, she would probably choose one of those you just saw."

His expression was suddenly very somber. After a long moment, he said, "Want some homemade strawberry pie?"

A little after one he pushed open the door of her house, standing behind her as she walked in. "What now?" he asked, walking inside.

She yawned and stretched her shoulders. "The sunshine, the food, the lack of sleep last night, has done me in. I think I'll take a short nap." She headed in the direction of the hall. "What about you?"

"Oh, I don't know. It's still early, so I may go on

up to the mountains for an hour or so. That is, unless you would like for me to take a nap with you," he said in a purely sensual tone.

She stopped dead and turned, her heart set to heavy pounding at his suggestion. She saw him move casually toward her. "Stop there," she ordered with a short laugh. "You have your own room. If you want to take a nap, take one in your own bed."

He stopped halfway across the room from her. His lips twisted and he sighed. "I don't suppose you want to hear my opposing argument?"

"No," she replied spritely. "You're much too sharp to stand there and waste your breath." With a parting smile she went on down the hall and entered her bedroom. With a single movement of her wrist she locked the door this time, not sure whether she was in fact, locking him out, or locking herself in. She peeled her dress off quickly and stepped out of it. Fifteen minutes later she was nestled in a sound sleep.

When she awoke she turned over and glanced at the time. Four o'clock. Rising quickly, she pulled her dress back on, listening for sounds of Mitch and hearing none. Moments later she discovered on the kitchen table a four-word note: "Gone to the mountains."

She stood pondering the words a minute, then walked to the living room and looked out to the drive. Her car was still where she had parked it at the return from the craft show. The second thing she pondered was how. How did he go? She had only the one car. For a moment all kinds of crazy thoughts swept her mind. Had he borrowed a car? If so, from whom? Had he contacted Charlotte and somehow gotten his car back from her? Or had he called Marsha?

She supposed she should be happy he wasn't there. But there was no fooling herself, she wasn't happy.

She sat at the table a long time, gazing at the note. On the way to her bedroom she opened the door to the room he occupied and peeked inside.

She looked around, finding the room was developing a new personality. On the dresser were his aftershave, deodorant, and bath powder. She eyed the shirt from yesterday folded neatly across the chair back over his worn trousers. She walked over to the dresser, lifted the bottle of aftershave, removed the top, and passed the bottle close to her nose a time or two. With a faint smile on her lips she replaced the top and put the bottle back.

Walking from the room, she pulled the door softly closed, giving the twin bed one involuntary last glance.

Before the remainder of the afternoon passed she had wished a thousand times she had gone with him instead of taking a nap. Before dusk she began preparing dinner, fully expecting him in by dark.

Dark came, dinner was ready and in the warmer, but no Mitch. Finally at eight o'clock she ate without him and placed his plate back into the warmer. A worried frown knitted her brows. How much of the mountains could be seen after dark, especially a moonless, starless night like the one outside?

She flipped on the TV and stretched out on the

sofa in the living room. She tried to concentrate on the screen, but her mind was going in mad circles. Troubled beyond concentration, she was angry with herself, angry with him, and very dissatisfied with the fact that she missed him and she wanted him home.

She rose, poured herself a glass of wine, and sat back down. Slowly she sipped.

At ten thirty she heard a car pull into her drive and a laughing "Thanks" followed by the slam of a door. The sound of his happy laughter completely set her off-balance. Here she had been for hours worried sick that he had driven off the side of one of the mountains, when most likely he had not given her a single thought while he was doing whatever he had been doing. One thing for certain, if he looked the least physically frayed when he walked through the door, she would kick his rear end right back out before he could blink his eyes.

As expected, he walked in like the king of humor, a wide smile on his lips, a twinkle in his blue eyes. "Hi," he said pleasantly, his smile broadening. "Miss me?"

She glared at him sullenly, but made no reply.

His smile did not waver, nor his eyes. "You didn't miss me," he stated matter-of-factly, answering his own question. With a sudden quick move of the hand, he rubbed his stomach. "I'm starved. Think I'll fix me something to eat."

As he took a single step toward the kitchen, she grunted begrudgingly, "Your dinner is in the warmer."

He halted and looked back to her. "You can

cook!" he declared with mocking jubilation.

She cut him the meanest glare she could manage. "No, I called in Julia Child."

Laughing under his breath, he walked out of the room. "Want to come in here with me?" he called through the wall.

"No, I don't," she replied huffily. "I'm watching a movie."

He laughed. "The news was on when I walked through there."

Her eyes shot quickly to the set and she saw the weather map stretched across the screen. Rolling her eyes upward, she grimaced.

"Say"—he was again in the doorway, glancing straight at her—"what are you doing drinking on Sunday?" Then he grinned slow and tauntingly. "Drowning your sins, or sorrows?"

Her lips pursed and her eyes narrowed. "I had no sorrows until yesterday morning," she said quietly. "As for my sins, I'm sure they won't warrant much attention when stacked beside someone like"—she paused dramatically, then added—"you."

He eyed her calmly, the grin still fixed on his lips. "Why are you trying to dampen my good mood?" he inquired softly. "I was happy to be back. I missed you."

She averted his eyes, thoughtfully put one finger to her lips, and turned her attention back to the television. When she heard him back in the kitchen, she picked up the glass of wine, turned it over, and emptied it. Before it had hit her stomach she was attacked by the hiccups. She hiccuped and the entire upper part of her body jerked spasmodically. Her hand flew to her mouth, covering it. Finally, after holding back the sounds until she had almost ripped out her lungs, she inhaled deeply and a loud *hic* erupted before she could stop it or close her mouth.

At that moment he walked in, bringing a glass of water, which he extended in her direction.

Her eyes were teary and red from the struggle as she looked up and muttered, "Thank you—*hic.*" She reached for the glass, but he set it on the table. In that same instant he had her in his arms, embracing her fiercely before she had time to realize what was happening. She cried, "Don't—*hic!*"

Quick as lightning he covered her mouth with an intense crushing kiss, his arms firm around her, his hands rubbing her back slowly, strongly.

Holding her breath, she stiffened in his arms, resisting the strength of his mouth holding her lips boldly captive.

All of a sudden he released her, drawing back with a sly grin on his lips. He tilted his head and whispered, "You're cured."

She was hardly breathing; in no way could she muster up a hiccup. He was grinning at her like he was the last of the miracle workers.

"That was the cure," he murmured seductively. "Now, here is the prevention." He kissed her softly on the mouth, extraordinarily gentle. And yet if his lips had been harsh molten lead, the effect would have been the same.

His arms held her tenderly as he kissed her over and over, intolerably soft, light brushes. Standing motionless, she sensed her very last resistance to him deserting her. She had fought his kisses, but the fight was ending. She wanted to kiss him.

Her mouth eased against his, her lips parted. Her arms slid up around his neck and crossed; her fingers shifted into his crisp hair.

His eyes blinked once, then closed tightly as his mouth opened. The barrier between them disappeared altogether when he pulled her close against him. Her breasts swelled against his chest; her heart clamored, rushing showers of sparks throughout her.

The tone of the kiss changed into a swift insistent rise of passion. Tongues touched and melted together as they floated down together onto the sofa. His mouth left hers and he kissed her neck with tiny wild hot brushes of his lips. The sparks were gathering, gathering into a vast flame burning deep within.

Her head twisted; her body writhed when his tongue swept along her ear. Her lips were on his neck, her hands on his shoulders, trembling, plying his flesh with long, tapered fingers. The flames inside were burning, fanned by the quickened hot breaths.

He pressed her back and leaned over her, covering her face and neck with darting, wild kisses. Suddenly she felt the palm of his hand beneath her skirt above her knee, making circling little paths as it traveled upward. She winced and grabbed his hand through her skirt, struggling to stop him. With a little cry she choked out, "No—Mitch."

He stopped and for a moment every sound disappeared. All was still. Slowly she opened her eyes and looked at him and motion came back into the room in the quick little shakes of her head.

His blue eyes clouded and he swallowed hard, an expression near agony on his face. His breathing remained shallow, ragged, as did hers for several long moments. Then he leaned forward to kiss her lips and she twisted her head slightly, allowing his mouth to linger on her cheek.

"Blair, why won't you," he whispered against her skin.

"I can't, Mitch," she answered softly. "Please, don't ask me to. I can't." She felt her eyes mist. She had not meant for it to come this far. She had only meant to kiss him. She knew he was hurting, but so was she. Still, she would not allow herself to soothe his hurt with her body, or soothe her own with his.

He studied her, his mouth moving before the words emerged painfully slow. "I don't know what to say, Blair." His voice was a dry whisper. "I suddenly feel seventeen again in the back seat of a car."

Her voice was as dry as his and as brittle. "Out with one of the uninhibited girls in school? Is that it?"

He paused and lifted one brow at her. "No." He gave a short laugh. "Those weren't the ones who always stopped me; it was the nice inhibited ones like you. And always when it was painful, just like now." He looked genuinely mystified when he added softly, "And I didn't understand any better at seventeen than I understand now at thirty-two. How do you cut your emotions off like that, Blair? It's like turning a faucet. It's like saying, 'You've had your sip, now, no more water.'"

Her darkened eyes locked on his. "Mitch, you give me too much credit or not enough, I don't know which. And I don't know that it matters. I am not inhibited, nor am I a water faucet. I am merely a woman who will not commit herself to the lovemaking act with a man who is little more than a stranger to her."

He was silent a moment, then said, "Desire makes strangers friends, don't you think?"

She thought a moment before saying, "Yes. Then when it's gone, burned up, burned out, the friends are strangers again."

He touched one hand to her cheek. "I'll bet you're tough in the courtroom, aren't you?" His fingers brushed across and touched her lips, then dropped away from her altogether.

Slowly he rose from the sofa, turned his back to her, straightened the legs of his trousers, tucked his shirt neatly back in at the waist, and flexed his back. He looked over his left shoulder to her, and with a morose laugh said, "Well, we did cure your hiccups, didn't we?"

"Yes," she answered. "We certainly did that."

He walked toward the door leading into the hallway, his hands in his pockets. Before leaving the room, he looked back at her, saying calmly, "This afternoon in the mountains I found myself thinking about you a lot, Blair. I found myself wondering about you and your Mr. Fairfield, wondering about your relationship with him." His lips twisted into a grin. "You're stalling with him, aren't you? The two of you are time killers."

70

"I don't know that it's any of your business, Mitch," she said after a short silence. "But Wayne and I are just friends."

"You aren't even that," he countered. "But you're right, it isn't any of my business. I just want you to know that it isn't going to be like that with us. No, indeed. We won't be time killers. And the only complaint we'll have about time is that there just won't be enough." His eyes glinted. "You're going to love me and I'm going to love you, and there isn't a whole lot either of us can do about it. Wait and see."

She smiled her disbelief, showing even white teeth. Making no reply to his remark, she asked, "How did you get to the mountains today, Mitch?"

"A friend," he answered without hesitation.

She was dying to ask whether it was male or female, but pride prevented such inquiry.

"It was nice," he went on. "There's nothing like it after a rain like last night's. The mist covering the deep valleys, the bright spring colors everywhere. We sat up on the overlook at six thousand feet and watched the clouds float by beneath us. Do you like the mountains, Blair?" he asked suddenly.

"I only like them from a distance. I don't care much about seeing them up close."

He nodded. "I wish you had gone with me."

After he had gone on down the hall, she sat in the living room, her hands clasped together, wondering why she also wished she had gone with him. Probably more than he wished it.

Finally she got up and turned off the lights in the front part of the house. Walking past his door, she hesitated, then called through the wall, "Don't bring me any apples tonight, Johnny Appleseed, I ate dinner."

He laughed and said, "Well, would you bring me one—I never did get around to mine."

She gave a delighted, throaty chuckle. "All right, I will," she said, and started on down the hall to the kitchen.

CHAPTER FIVE

The next morning she drove him to his sheetrock company on the outer edge of town before driving in to her office. It was a large metal building with offices in the front part constructed of glass and brick. The building and yard were enclosed by a chain link fence and gate which he unlocked before she could drive him inside.

Pulling up in front of the office, she halted and asked, "Did you keep an operation going here while you were gone, Mitch?"

He nodded. "Yes. One crew did stay here and work mainly on small contracts, houses, renovations —that type of thing. But we should be back in full swing in a couple of weeks now that construction has picked up. I plan to buy a new fleet of vehicles today, including my own set of wheels."

A car drove through the front gate and she cut a quick glance, but was disappointed to see a man behind the wheel. Then she went back to her conversation with Mitch. "You think I might look around?" she asked, lifting her brows.

He smiled. "Sure thing. Come on in."

For the next twenty minutes she walked with him while he explained the operations of the company. From the corners of her eyes she kept a surveillance of the gates, waiting for Marsha Partlow to make an appearance. Finally she commented, "Not many people have shown up for work, have they?" She glanced at her watch. "It's almost nine o'clock."

He looked at her strangely for a moment, then smiled and said, "That's because those who were out of the country with me are on vacation for the next week." His tongue swirled around his teeth slowly and he asked dryly, "Are you looking for anyone in particular?"

"No," she said quickly, coolly. She walked over to the brown metal file cabinet, and as she touched the side with two fingers, she rounded her mouth and said low, "Nice."

He laughed bitterly. "Don't tell Charlotte; she'll drive over in my little car and load it up."

A weird sensation struck her. As things now stood there was a good possibility she could wind up in court again representing Charlotte Morgan—against Mitch. Startled, she opened her mouth, saying, "Mitch, are you going to see an attorney today?"

He smiled ruefully. "Do you have to ask, Blair?"

Ten minutes later she walked into her own offices to find Lynn coming out of her private door, a dustcloth in her hand. "Good morning," she said brightly.

"Morning, Lynn," Blair said softly. "Have there been any calls?"

Lynn laughed easily. "Not from *him,* if that's what you're worried about."

Blair looked around with uncertainty. "Wha— what?" came her puzzled response.

Lynn seated herself behind her desk, not taking her eyes from Blair. "The caller from Friday, the man who was so angry." She shook her head. "He hasn't called."

Blair responded half under her breath, "I know, but has anyone else called?"

Lynn shook her head. "No. It's been unusually quiet for a Monday. I started with the cleaning. I stacked last week's files on your desk for any final notations you might want to make before I put them away."

Blair extended her hand for the dustcloth. "Thanks. I'll finish. Maybe next term of court we can be neater. Maybe you won't have to spend all week out of the office running last-minute errands."

Lynn passed her the cloth somewhat reluctantly. "Blair," she said hesitantly, "is anything wrong?"

Blair reached her door and looked back. "Tell me, Lynn," she began slowly, thoughtfully, "of last week's cases, did any of them strike you as being—uh —somewhat out of the ordinary? When you typed the briefs did any particular one stay in your mind?"

Lynn bit her lower lip fiercely. "Uhmmm, two come to mind right off. The Cliffords, mainly because of their ages." She smiled. "Forty years was a long time to live with an incompatible mate." She paused. "And the Morgans. I found it difficult to understand how a man could give up such a fabulous home, expensive car, all that money in the joint bank accounts, to run off with his secretary. I don't understand that kind of passionate love, I suppose. Terry wouldn't do it. And he's the least materialistically inclined person I know. Even with the kids, I don't think he would give it all up." Suddenly she raised her brows. "I don't think I would expect him to, but Mrs. Morgan did. From what little I saw of her she seemed to be very bitter. And very cold. Was it either of those you had in mind?" she asked solemnly.

Without saying a word Blair nodded thoughtfully, then opened the door to her office and entered slowly. She dropped the cloth on top of the bookcase and went behind her desk and sat down. Before she had reached for a single folder, a quick tap sounded on the door and Lynn slipped inside, her hazel eyes round and surprised. "Blair, this is the strangest thing. You know who just walked in?"

Blair looked up and said, her voice as emotionless as her face, "Charlotte Morgan."

Lynn nodded. "That's right." She cocked her head. "Were you expecting her?"

Blair smiled secretively and explained, "Let's just say I'm not surprised, Lynn. Please send Mrs. Morgan in."

A minute later she was looking directly into the half-lidded eyes of Charlotte Morgan, a mature, tall shapely woman with elevated thin brows on a pretty round face that expressed discomfort at the moment. She was dressed neatly in a clinging red dress, and for an instant, looking at her, Blair thought, *He loved her. At one time Mitch loved this woman sitting across from me.* The thought gave her a funny feeling in the pit of her stomach.

She pulled closer to her desk, leaned forward, and asked, "What can I do for you this morning, Mrs. Morgan?" Not knowing what to expect, she inhaled and sat back in the leather chair.

Charlotte considered a moment, then said in a cool unemotional tone, "My ex-husband is back in town."

Blair gave a single nod. "And?"

Charlotte shifted in her chair, then went on. "I think he's probably going to make some problems for me, that is, if he can."

Blair's brows rose and she pursued the subject. "How is that?" She watched Charlotte's fingers clamp together before offering, "He may contest the divorce. Can he do that?"

Blair's eyes fixed on the gray-green ones. "No," she replied very softly. "The time for that was before the court decree was handed down. But, tell me, why do you think he might enter into any type of action now. He had a year to reply. Why now?"

Much to her surprise Charlotte replied without hesitation. "He's been out of the country for the past year working in Saudi Arabia. I didn't know," she said quietly, convincingly. "He didn't bother to tell me. Now that he's back he's decided he was too generous. He wants his"—she corrected herself—"*the* house back, along with the Jaguar, some of the money, and other minor things. He's going to put on this big act that he didn't transfer any of those deeds and titles to me. He says I forged his name."

Blair sat silent a moment, trying to absorb what

she was hearing. Finally she asked straight out, "Did you?"

Charlotte wasted no time in saying, "No. An analysis of the signatures will verify the writing is his. But he's had all these months to think over his actions and now he wants to renege."

Blair sat in shock. Either Charlotte Morgan was the most convincing liar ever born, or the woman was telling the truth.

Charlotte's eyes glinted with a spurt of anger. She went on. "He didn't want to be married to me; he wanted his freedom—at any price. Now he has it, but he's decided the price was too high. And I have no intention of giving him back a single thing—not the least. I'm here because I want you to be aware of these developments and take whatever steps are indicated to prevent him from harassing me."

Blair touched her forehead thoughtfully and frowned. Somehow she had to remove herself from this entire mess. It was going to become messier in the days ahead.

Charlotte talked on. "It's possible he or his attorney will contact you, and I wanted you to know what's going on. Also, I wanted to have an inkling into what his attorney could do. What can they do?" She ended with the abrupt question.

Blair placed her hands on top of her desk and inhaled deeply. "If the question of fraud is presented to Judge Walker and evidenced, then the entire divorce action will be set aside. The court will nullify it and a new action will have to be instigated."

Charlotte smiled for the first time since entering the office. "You mean, we won't be divorced?"

Blair gave an affirmative nod. "Not by that decree."

Charlotte gave a throaty chuckle. "I would love to see his face when his attorney puts that to him. Even if he wins, he loses." She rose to leave, the grin lingering on her lips. "And Marsha loses. I would almost be willing to admit I forged his signatures to see that happen."

After Charlotte had gone, Blair sank deeper into the cushioned shelter of the chair. She could not fathom what had happened in this case. It smacked of something terrible, something unreal. She needed the truth. But what was it? Thoughts raced through her mind. For the first time in her life she felt near stupid. She had never been a pushover for a good-looking face, but Mitchell Morgan's had come close —too close—to pushing her over. She wanted to make sure he got out of her house today.

Frantically she looked up the number of Morgan Sheetrock and dialed nervously. A man answered, telling her that Mitch was gone for the day. She twisted her head, fiercely thinking that he had better be looking for a place to live because if he hadn't, come nightfall he would find himself and his luggage out on her front porch. This thing could balloon so that she could find herself in front of an ethics committee before it was over if she didn't watch her step very closely.

She stared straight ahead into the air. She was still staring when Lynn stuck her head in the door and said, "Blair, Mrs. Cobb is here. Are you ready for her?"

Blair stared at her emptily, and after a passing second nodded.

Lynn stepped aside and a young teary-eyed woman in her early twenties walked in. Before the door had closed tears began pouring down the young cheeks and she said between sobs, "Miss Bennett . . . I—I want to file . . . for a divorce."

For some reason Blair felt like crying with her.

Late that afternoon Lynn came into the office with a long, typed page and put it on the desk. "Here's Mrs. Cobb's complaint," she said unusually softly. "How do young girls like her get in such a mess?"

Looking up, Blair answered, "There is no mystery here, Lynn. The explanation is really quite simple. A brute standing up is a brute lying down. Basic personalities don't change when pajamas are put on. What's simpler than that?"

A sad smile covered Lynn's face. "You know, Blair, the longer I work here the more I value my own marriage. It's not perfect, but it is workable. If only Terry could overcome his jealousy. Oh, well," she said lightly, "after typing something like this, I realize he's nearly perfect, even with that little streak. I think I'll keep him." She cleared her throat and hesitated. "Uh—you didn't put anything on my desk concerning the first client of the day, Charlotte Morgan." Again she paused. "Was there anything?"

Blair gave a rigid shake of her head. "No. But the validity of that divorce is in question. . . ." Her words trailed off.

Lynn gazed at Blair, puzzled. "From the grin on

that woman's face when she left, I would say she isn't worried."

"Maybe not," Blair snapped. "Maybe she's transferred all the worry to other shoulders."

Lynn said nothing to that as she slowly turned and left the office.

Blair tried to reach Mitch one last time before leaving for home. No luck. The best she could hope for was that he had already picked up his belongings and left her house.

She felt a knot curl in her stomach when she turned onto her street and saw a new car parked in her drive. It was a strange knot, tied with mixed emotions. She was both happy and angry to see the car. Walking past it, she hardly gave it a glance.

Her heartbeat increased into a snappier pace, and when she pushed open the front door, her mouth fell with surprise. There just inside was his luggage waiting to be carried out. Swiftly her gaze went to the living room where Mitch was rising to his feet. She swung about to face him.

"Hi," he said with a soft smile.

"Hello," she said gently, unsmilingly, and pushed the door closed. "I see you bought yourself a car," she blurted out.

He nodded.

Feeling strangely lost, she realized it was not easy to look at him.

"And an apartment," he added, walking toward her. "I was advised to get my own place until the matter is settled."

She brushed one side of her hair with her fingers.

81

"I hope you didn't tell where you had stayed over the weekend."

He gave a low laugh. "No, I'm smarter than that. I merely said I was staying with a friend." With a slight shrug he teased, "Was I?"

She gave a quick shake. "I don't know how we can be friends, Mitch. Not now, not under the circumstances. Maybe someday when all this is settled."

His blue eyes traveled over her face. "Blair, we are friends. Whether or not you admit it, we are. We're friends because we care about each other. And in the very near future we're going to be lovers, whether or not you admit it."

Her eyes darkened and narrowed at him. She swallowed. "Those odds are very slight; as a matter of fact, that possibility is nonexistent. The most sensible thing we can do is say good-bye and good luck, and let it go at that. I am in a most uncomfortable situation as a result of these past days and my career and my life are things I value very highly." Even as she spoke she could feel the longings they shared as they stood apart. Even not touching she could feel it.

They faced each other silently, as if in some kind of mental duel.

"I've thought about you all day, Blair," he said in a somewhat leaden voice. "I haven't been able to put you from my mind."

She put up one hand and said unhappily, "Just don't, Mitch. Don't say words like those to me. I don't want to hear them."

"Even if it's the truth?"

Abruptly her eyes widened. "The truth, Mitch? Are we about to speak of truths? Because if we are, then let's do." She breathed in quickly. "The truth is you don't give a damn about me, except the damn you give about sleeping with me. You want to make love to me—and that's the truth! The fact that I am the attorney who represented your former wife is another truth. And maybe the truth is that if somehow you overpower me, her attorney, you will have overpowered her. The truth is that I was stupid to allow you in, and the last truth is, I am happy to see you go."

For a moment she couldn't read his expression. Anger, fury, defeat, surprise, and then the last she didn't expect. He smiled, a slow curve of his lips turning upward before he said, "Not guilty of the first charge, or the second. Guilty of the third, not guilty of the fourth or fifth. And for your record, it's not stupid to show compassion, and your last truth is a lie. You are as happy to see me go as I am in leaving. The truth is, when I came to your house I had no intention of staying here; the thought had not crossed my mind. But with only two cabs in town, the driver could not wait for me because he had a regular customer to take to the beauty shop. I removed my luggage because I had some important documents inside that I couldn't risk losing. I was in the process of switching hotels, so that I would be closer to my business. But when I met you, Blair, when I saw you, I didn't want to leave. I came by here out of anger because you refused to answer my call on Friday. But I stayed simply because I didn't want to leave. I know it wasn't smart, but it wasn't the dumbest thing I've ever done—and I don't regret doing it." He moved over to his bags and lifted them from the floor. "I suppose I'll be seeing you in court, won't I?"

She stood in silence, watching him walk toward the door. Then she moved over to open it for him, and as she reached out he stopped dead still and looked at her. Then he lowered the bags again to the floor. Tenderly his eyes went over her face and he said, "It's going to be a long time before this moment comes again. I want to kiss you, Blair."

She shook her head. "No," she whispered. She knew better than to kiss him, to allow him to kiss her. Her insides were already at a frantic pitch and one touch from him would be her undoing. "Please just go, Mitch," she implored. "Everything that needs to be said has been. Let's leave it here at this."

Slowly his eyes left hers, and without another word he walked out the door.

CHAPTER SIX

She stood motionless, looking at the closed door, her eyes opened wide, her face a sudden retreat for loneliness. Finally she turned away and left the foyer, her steps accompanied by an inner voice whispering, *You did the only thing you could. He had to go.*

Perhaps, sometime later, they could meet again. Later, after all this was settled. Up until this moment she had not realized that the wait could be lonely as well as long, drawn out over weeks, even months. At any rate, she had the distinct feeling she had just seen Mitch Morgan exit from her life.

The remainder of the week passed and her feeling about him proved correct. He made no attempt to contact her in any way, not a call, nothing. On Saturday evening Wayne came over and the two of them cooked dinner over the backyard grill. Leaving him outside to tend the steaks, she went inside to toss a salad. Standing at the counter, she looked out the window as she pulled the lettuce into small pieces. Wayne was seated in a lawn chair near the grill, the fall of night settling around him. The sun had edged past the horizon and the deep tones of red were fading like wispy fingers into the emerging deep blue that would soon cover the state of Virginia.

Looking at Wayne, she could no longer see him clearly. She could see only Mitch. It was strange to look at one man and see another.

When she had finished with the salad, she covered the bowl and slid it into the refrigerator, then walked back out onto the patio and called, "About done?"

Wayne turned his head to her. "Another minute or so," he replied factually, leaning forward in his chair. "What happened to your uncle, Blair?" he asked suddenly.

She felt the flush start low in her neck and blaze upward. "Wayne," she began, "he wasn't my uncle. I don't know why I felt the need to lie about him. He wasn't a relative at all." She gave a tiny shrug of her shoulders. "He was just a man."

Wayne sat rigid in his chair. His expression became one of sheer disbelief. "I would think there's more explanation than that, Blair. What was he doing staying the night at your house?"

"Could we not discuss it, please," she spluttered. "I'm sure you wouldn't understand."

"That's right," he snapped in a voice totally new to her. "I don't understand. I don't understand what he was doing here, or why you would lie to me about him. Blair, I've taken such care to treat you as the lady I thought you were." His eyes suddenly rounded. "I don't know you at all, do I?"

"I'm not involved with him, if that's what you're thinking," she said.

"I don't know what I'm thinking, except maybe some kind of fool is sitting in this chair!" he exclaimed loudly, jumping to his feet. "A week ago, Blair, I left you with a man in his pajamas. A man I was told was a relative, and now you tell me he isn't related to you. I'm certainly no expert on the law, but the evidence seems to be a bit overwhelming against you, Blair. Unless you can offer some explanation with a little more substance, I'm not sure I want to continue our relationship. I'm not sure we should."

A bright flame burst on the grill and the two steaks were engulfed. Overhead a single star had pierced the dark heavens. She looked forlornly at the blazing grill, then at the shining star that seemed to be twinkling a kind of remote laughter at the scene taking place in her backyard. "Wayne," she said quite emotionless, "the steaks just burned up."

He strode past her, slapping the fork into her hand as he passed by. "That's not all that just burned up here, Blair." He jerked the patio door and declared under his breath, "I'll never learn . . ."

She didn't follow him. She stood on the patio until she heard his car squeal from her drive, then she turned on the hose and drenched the fire in the grill. When it was out, she turned off the hose, gathered up the utensils, and started into the house. She looked back at the grill and saw that Duchess had crossed the yard and was sitting on the ground, sniffing the charred air. She walked back, lifted the burned steaks with the tongs, and placed both at the dog's feet. "Have a feast, girl," she whispered.

During the short walk back to the house she found herself thinking that if it was possible, as some believed, for the earth and heavens to come together in the brief span of seven days, it was equally possible for her life to come apart in the same number of days. But, actually, it hadn't taken seven, only two. Last weekend. And now, add tonight. Three. With Wayne's departure from her life she found herself with two fears; one, that she wouldn't miss him; the other, that she wouldn't stop missing Mitch.

With a bolt of unexpected energy she cleaned her house for the next hour. She stayed busy with the chores she most hated; cleaning out the refrigerator, scrubbing the stove until the enamel sparkled, spraying the oven, then closing the door to allow a miracle to take place. While the oven cleaned she moved into the living room and began to remove books from the shelves, where she worked slowly, dusting each book.

Sitting in the floor, legs folded under her, she was removing tiny particles from the tops of the pages when she heard the car drive up. The sound of steps on the porch brought her slowly to her feet. Wayne must have come back. No doubt with an apology for his temperamental backyard inquisition.

The doorbell rang and she took her time in answering. She wasn't sure that anything else needed to be said between Wayne and herself. Somewhat unsure of what she intended to say, she opened the door.

She looked into Mitch's unsmiling face. The tiny laugh lines about his eyes and mouth were smooth, a part of an expression she had never seen on his face.

If anything, he looked glum. He was dressed in burgundy cotton trousers, a lightweight plaid sport coat with a stripe in it that matched the pants, and a white dress shirt open at the collar. She knew he was seeing her barefoot, in faded denims, cotton shirt hanging almost to her knees, with sleeves rolled to her elbows; clothes she had thrown on before she started cleaning. She felt a bit uneasy about the way she must look to him. "Hello," she finally managed.

His voice sounded unusually rigid when he replied, "I took a chance on finding you home." His lips turned upside down. "No Saturday night date?"

"It ended early," she said, biting her lip. "I'm in the middle of cleaning."

He took a single step and reached out, clasping her arm lightly. "I've come to kidnap you. The cleaning will have to wait."

The sudden hammering in her chest disturbed her to the point she twisted free of his touch. "No," she insisted, somewhat unsteadily. "The kidnapping will have to wait."

He smiled and the lines came back to his mouth and eyes. "You know, counsellor, I thought the time I spent overseas was a long time, but it was a fleeting second in comparison to this past week. Now I am on your doorstep to tell you the week has ended and you have two choices. I will either stay here with you, or you can come with me. And I think your safer option is to come with me."

"No," she whispered. "The safest option is for you to leave. We both know that."

His smile widened. "But, darling, that one isn't available. Why don't you get your shoes on before my caveman genes take over and I throw you across my shoulder and haul you off into the night with your toes dangling."

She touched her blouse, saying, "I can't go anywhere looking like this." She raised her arm and turned slightly, displaying a long rip at the sleeve and shoulder seam.

He came closer, a mockingly sinister glint in his blue eyes. "You're stalling, and it isn't working."

She put down her arm and looked up at him. "And you're bluffing," she said with a sure smile. "If my life in court has taught me anything, it's to know a bluff when I hear one. You're much too intelligent to kidnap any woman, least of all a woman of the law—"

The word *like* emerged in a shriek when he swooped her up in the air and over his shoulder. Holding her tightly around the legs with one hand, he reached out and pulled the door closed with the other, then turned and started quickly down the steps.

"Put me down!" she screeched. "Mitch! My neighbors!" She stiffened, her waist at his shoulder, her upper body straightening in mid-air. Her hands clasped his back.

He reached the car, opened the door, and lowered her to the concrete on his side. He nudged her inside with a firm hold on her hips, then climbed in close behind her.

Her mouth fell open when he started the motor and backed from the drive. "Mitch . . . I didn't get my shoes!" she half-wailed in a splutter. "Or change my clothes!"

90

His arm squeezed around her shoulder and he laughed with delight. "You had your chance, but being the keen-eyed lady lawyer you are, you detected the bluff." He halted at the four-way stop at the end of her street and looked at her. His hand moved from her shoulder up to the side of her neck and face, his fingers sliding lightly into her hair. Drawing her near, his mouth covered hers softly.

The touch of his lips slayed whatever will power she had hidden inside in reserve for the hours ahead. In that moment her lips became obsessed with his and she returned his kiss passionately. Lightning touched her lips and ran through her body, leaving her with a glow that suddenly made her feel naked, exposed.

The effect of her response on him was immediate and he moaned, releasing her mouth, only to recapture it in a caress less gentle than the first.

The sound of a car horn behind them made him draw away abruptly.

She looked at him, but found she couldn't say anything. He turned the car right, in the direction of the interstate. His arm was around her neck and he drew her face to the side of his own. "How would you like to go to the mountains with me, counsellor? Like the top of Skyline Drive?"

"The mountains! Tonight!" She gave a single shake of her head. "I can't do that. Good heavens, Mitch, it would be midnight before we got there. And I don't have on my shoes. It'll be cold up there!"

A slow smile curved his lips. "What if I promise you won't be cold?"

She pulled away from his arm, slid to her side of

the seat, then turned her body toward him. "What have you done, rented a cabin?" she asked.

His hands tightened on the steering wheel. Slowly he nodded, then reluctantly admitted, "Yes."

Her head tilted and her mouth parted as she glared at him. "That was a tad presumptuous, wasn't it?" Her eyes grew larger. "I'm not spending the night in any cabin with you. Your fondness of the mountains is yours alone. I don't like them. I don't like those narrow roads, or those dangerous heights, and most certainly I don't like staying in a cabin with bears and all kinds of wild creatures peering in the windows. So you just turn this car around and head back to civilization. Right now!"

His chin dropped, his face tightening in a grimace. "What if I tell you it has two bedrooms? Would that make a difference?"

"No," she said, looking over at him. "If it had six you still only intend to make use of one." Even as she spoke he took the exit from the interstate leading up to the Drive across the Shenandoahs. Completely baffled, she said loudly, "Didn't you hear me, Mitch! I'm not going! If you drive me to any cabin in this wilderness against my will, you're going to be in serious trouble!"

"Blair," he said softly, lifting his chin. "You remind me of myself when I was a child and my mother tried to get me to the dentist. I would declare until the last moment I wasn't going. Even when she had my arm, dragging me out the door, I would still declare I wasn't going. All the way there I would swear I wasn't going to get out of the car. It always took me sitting there in that chair to realize I'd lost

92

my battle. But, after all, here I am, thirty-two with all my teeth, thanks to my mother."

She rolled her eyes to the top of the car. "That's a touching analogy, Mitch, but if you think I see the connection between that situation and this, you're mistaken. I don't believe you've rented a cabin to check my teeth."

He chuckled and paused a moment. "You did miss the point, darling. It's possible at some time you may be happy I forced my will upon you. I'm a lot like my mother in that respect."

She sat quite still, rubbing her toes hard into the carpet of his new car. Obviously he wasn't going to turn around as she requested.

She peered through the windshield at the narrow winding road ahead and felt her insides shriveling. Clasping her hands together in her lap, she sighed heavily. Keeping a close watch on the road, she did not risk talking for fear she would avert his attention and plunge them over the mountainside. Only a full-fledged idiot would kidnap an attorney. Releasing her hands, she pulled the seat belt across her and fastened it.

He smiled and said softly, "I am determined to get you there safely."

"That's good," she grunted. "Because I am probably going to have to send you to prison, and I'll need to be in one piece."

"What's the charge?" he chuckled, not attempting to hide his amusement.

"Kidnapping," she replied haughtily, then added, "for a start."

He laughed aloud. "For a start. Sounds like if I'm

lucky I can carve my name along with the infamous —Baby Face Nelson, Al Capone, Legs Diamond, Crazy Mitch Morgan." He raised one hand from the wheel and made little dashes through the air, saying, "Crazy Mitch kidnaps former wife's attorney and hides her away in remote mountain cabin for a week where he tortured her unmercifully with love. Crazy Mitch, headed for a new kind of chair."

"Put your hand back on that wheel!" she exclaimed with alarm. She looked at him, then at length asked threateningly, "And what do you mean, a week!"

A tiny shrug and an innocent, "Seven days?"

"Oh, no," she protested strongly. "If you think I'm about to spend seven days with you in an isolated cabin, you have just earned your new name! I have clients, I have a law practice, and I will definitely be in my office Monday morning."

He tried to hide a grin from her when he said softly, "Agreed. I'll have you back by Monday."

It took a moment for her to realize she had fallen into that one head first. In retaliation she said, almost in a whisper, "I am not going to share your bed, Mitch. Understand me now, before we get to that cabin. I cannot. It's conceivable that unless I can remove myself as Charlotte's attorney, I may face you in the courtroom. And I don't know how I can do that if we've been intimate."

He sighed helplessly. "Okay, Blair. I won't offer you any argument. But at least we will have this time alone. Who knows, maybe you'll come to like the mountains."

Suddenly he slowed the car and pulled into the

parking area of an overlook. He reached across the seat and lifted a small tote bag, unzipped it, and removed a pair of cotton socks. "Give me your feet," he said with a smile.

She reached for the socks. "I can put them on," she returned.

He held the socks back from her grasp. "Your feet are my responsibility."

She extended one leg to him and when his hands closed around her foot she felt his fingers making slow circles on her skin until she could feel the warmth spread up her body.

She jerked her foot away and grabbed the socks from his hand. "I'll take those!" she snapped loudly. "My feet are *my* responsibility!" Quickly she pulled on both socks and placed her feet down. "Now, let's go. I don't like being parked on this cliff."

Half-shifted in her direction, his blue eyes gazed solemnly at her. "Want to get out and take a look? It's beautiful, one of the most beautiful sights on earth."

"I can see all I want to see from right here," she declared, giving a quick sweep out the window. "If you gave me the socks so I can get out in this black night and look down into blackness and up into blackness and tell you I see some kind of beauty out there that I don't see, then you can have your damned socks back. I'm not getting out of this car." Her eyes blazed across at him. "And don't you touch me that way again. I know what you're trying to do. It won't work."

"What way?" he inquired with too much bewilderment to be believable.

"Do you really think I don't know what you were doing when you drew those sweet little circles on my feet with your fingers?"

He took one of her hands and held it between his. Then he began to caress the top with the same slow motions of his fingers as he had done to her foot. "Like this?" he said, trying to keep back his smile. Slowly he turned her hand and tenderly kissed her palm. "I would have done this," he whispered between kisses, "except you pulled your foot away." He planted a last kiss in her palm, then lifted his eyes. "Why did you kiss me at the four-way stop?"

She tried to sound flippant. "Because I thought it was safe. Few people make love at four-way stop signs; usually there isn't time." She knew she should remove her hand from his grip, but it remained quite fixed in his.

His brows rose. "Then I am to believe that you aren't opposed to a 'safe kiss?' Is that right?" His tone became suggestively soft. "Like, for instance, if we should kiss here on this cliff, it would be safe, don't you think?"

Her own voice sounded unusually husky when she whispered, "There's no such thing as a 'safe' one now, not dangling from a cliff, or hanging in a tree, and certainly not locked up together in a cabin."

"Oh, I agree," he said quickly. "Absolutely not in the cabin. Once we walk inside we'll quarantine our lips." He smiled into her eyes. "But I'm talking about here, now, where it's safe."

She gazed at him wonderingly. Her tongue touched her upper lip briefly, thoughtfully. "All right, Mitch, but this is the last time until we get back to town."

He eased forward and his fingers touched her hair. She tensed, her breath caught involuntarily. Lips had yet to meet, still she felt the deadly tremble and knew in that instant her hunger was as great as his. Knowing that, she tried to avert her face, turn her lips from his. Powerful hands in her hair prevented the move.

He kissed her forehead, her closed lids, his mouth making a slow path to her lips. Her eyes opened and she looked exploringly at his face so close to hers, at his straight nose, his dark, beautifully shaped eyebrows, at lashes long and black, at lips exquisitely perfect and full. Feeling a sudden alarm, she backed from him and breathed quickly. "No." Her mind was racing wildly.

He kissed a corner of her mouth, moving slowly across until his lips covered hers. Her eyes flickered once more, then closed. Every sensation inside her drew her to him. His lips crushed brazenly on her, twisting, circling, until she could no longer breathe, merely gasp. Her arms wrapped around his head in the wake of unrecognizable passion.

He groaned against her lips and her mouth wandered open. His tongue caressed hers until her body was desire-wracked, until she could feel nothing but the fierce warmth enslaving her. He drew away only far enough to reach the buttons on her blouse, slowly releasing her, freeing her until she was completely exposed from the waist up.

His arms went around her and he held her up, his lips at the soft hollow of her throat. Instinctively she tensed, straightening higher as his lips underwent the journey from her neck downward, burning her flesh everywhere he touched, then softened when he reached one of her breasts, tasting, teasing, consuming her over and over as if he could never get enough, until her entire body glowed like a ruby.

Her hands were on his shoulders, in his hair, running up and down along his neck. She was unaware of how dry her mouth had become. She tossed her head, gasping for a deep breath. In that instant she loved him, she hated him. Loved him for his tenderness, the gentleness that made her ecstatic; hated him for making her wanton, desperate, for making her a prisoner to need.

His lips kissed the flat surface of her stomach downward to the waist of her jeans. He drew back quickly and slipped from his shirt in a particularly adept move. In the next instant he pressed his naked chest to hers and his arms caught around her, pulling her across so that she straddled his legs. At some point unknown to her, he had reclined the seat.

His hands slid downward, releasing, pushing back the faded jeans until her hips were bare and shining white in the moonlight that had appeared from behind a layer of clouds to take away the dark harbor of their passion.

She was awakened to the powerful quivering of his flesh, to the hard physical yearning still tightly contained within his clothing. She pressed against him, torturing him, hypnotizing him as a flame does a moth. Desire stirred his words thickly, blurred sounds slipping past her into the night. Slowly, surely, she moved over him, not freeing him, but holding him captive, bearing down on him with all her strength in relentless pressure that was shattering him. For fleeting moments she felt a thrill of power, the power of the flame burning the moth, making him a helpless subject to her will. He could do nothing.

Her arms went around his neck, her fingers gripping his back. His breathing was hoarse and quick. His mouth opened and she covered it with hers, her tongue playing with his teeth, his lips, delicately moving and pressing his. He was like granite, hot granite, and she clung to him with such force, showering his mouth, his face, with kisses.

He strained wildly against her and with one precise move she found herself swept under him. Out in the dark, somewhere on the mountainside below them, she heard the lonely cry of a wild creature. His naked legs, his naked, flat, dark nipples flashed at her in the white light coming at them through the trees.

She watched him sink down to her, bending slowly forward. She heard her own single word escape into the silence. "Mitch . . ." He drew closer and covered her. It was a sensation like no other and when the devouring flame claimed her, she wondered how it was, or when it was, that she had become the moth.

For a long time she lay in his embrace, not speaking, her senses dulled, her arms and legs limp, her body destroyed by passion already struggling to rebuild itself. His head was relaxed above her shoulder, his face pressing into her soft damp curls.

Suddenly her mood changed from ecstasy to anger. Something inside her made her want to strike out at him. She was choking on her own emotions. She gasped harshly. "I'm sure that your dreams as a seventeen-year-old have now been realized. Are you satisfied!"

"Uhmmm," he whispered close to her ear. "All my dreams have been realized." Bending down, he kissed her shoulder softly. "And I'm happy, too, in case you're wondering."

She struggled in his arms. She still felt as though he were crushing her to death. "Please remove yourself; I want to get my clothes on."

He sat up, peering at her face carefully. "I adore you, Blair," he said with a chuckle in his voice. "You aren't going to act as though I took advantage of you, are you?"

Her hands flattened against his shoulders, pushing him back from her. Anger made her stronger than ever; anger at herself, but more at him. She fumed. "For God's sake, Mitch, I am only human. You have been trying to accomplish this since the moment I first met you, and now you've done it. I'm glad you're satisfied—and *happy*."

He moved to his side of the car, freeing her to start yanking her clothes back in place, muttering under her breath, "I can't believe we allowed ourselves . . . irresponsibility, that's what it was. No, worse than that, like two over-aged adolescents tearing at each other in a damned car . . . oh . . ." She sighed aloud. "I just can't believe it." She angrily pressed the button on her side and her seat came back to an upright position. Bending over, she ripped the socks from her feet and flung them at him. "My feet *weren't* cold, in case you're interested. And this isn't going to happen again, just in case you're planning ahead!"

His smile was toothy and secure as he reached out and dropped the socks back onto her lap. "You might want to keep these then."

Her eyes rounded and flashed at him. "You might as well give up and take me back to my home. I know you're thinking that now, now that we've done *this*, we'll do it again. But I'm telling you, Mitch, we *won't*." She turned her face to the window and heaved a long sigh. Her eyes widened grotesquely large as she looked down past the low brick barrier to the valley below, now visible in the pale moonlight. Her head snapped around at him and she shrieked, "We're forty miles straight up!"

"Blair, darling," he said calmly, starting the motor. "We're six thousand feet. Please, don't excite yourself," he chided her with a soft chuckle. "You just saw what happens when you get excited." He pulled out into the drive, his right hand reaching blindly for hers.

She drew away and folded her fingers across each other, burying them between her knees. "Oh, no, you don't," she stated matter-of-factly. "You'll be drooling all over yourself before you touch me again."

In less than five minutes he turned into a narrow rock road that traveled up the western side of a mountain. A minute later he pulled to a stop in front of a small stone-and-log cabin. Her hand flew to her mouth and she gasped around her fingers. "Is this it!"

"Yes," he replied softly. "Like it?"

"You—you—idiot!" she exclaimed wildly. "You mean we made love hanging on that ledge when we were this close to the cabin!" She closed her eyes and shook her head, hoarsely whispering, "You must be demented. No sane person on earth would do something like that."

His long fingers touched the door handle as he faced her. "I love you, Blair, and nothing you've said, or anything you might say, is going to change that. I love you."

She leaped out her door and glared over the car top at him. "I expected you to say those exact words. Now that we're alone on this godforsaken mountain, at this godforsaken cabin, what else could you be expected to say?"

He stood motionless a moment, a grin covering his lips, then locking into place as he said softly, "I could be expected to say, 'Want to go in or stand out here yelling and squealing until you run off all the bears?'"

Her mouth dropped, then opened slightly when she whispered, rolling her eyes to the corners, "Are there really bears out here?"

He walked around the car, swept her up in his strong arms, and whispered into the side of her neck, "Grrrrr."

To which she mocked, "I already knew about that one."

CHAPTER SEVEN

The night had been warm in the town at the edge of the mountains, but the cabin several thousand feet above sea level was very cool. When Mitch lowered her from his arms to the stone floor, she stood a moment, then dashed to the thick rug in the middle of the room.

"I'll get some heat going," he said evenly, his eyes sparkling with laughter.

She stared at him and wrapped her arms around herself. Then her gaze turned abruptly to the cabin. It was a single large rectangular room with living area, kitchen, and sleeping area all combined. To the right of where she stood was a stove, refrigerator, table, sink, and cabinets. Directly to the left were two full-size beds placed side by side. She glared at him suspiciously. "Are those the two bedrooms?" she asked sharply, freeing one hand from under an arm to point in the direction of the beds.

103

He looked back over his shoulder from where he knelt at the fireplace and grinned. "Yes. One for you and one for me." His brows raised innocently. "What's the matter, don't you like them?" He returned to the job of starting the fire. "You can have your choice."

She tensed and muttered, "I should have expected as much." She wandered over to the refrigerator and opened the door. Her eyes widened with surprise when she found it well-stocked with every imaginable item. Holding the door open, she stared across to him again. "This was a well-planned abduction, wasn't it? There's enough food here to feed an army."

He did not stir from his position. "Not an army," he laughed good-naturedly, "just two love-starved people."

Dismayed, she slammed the door and her eyes swept the ceiling. "Who owns this cabin?" she inquired coolly.

She watched as he started up to his feet and ventured a step in her direction. He answered softly, "A former sheetrock tycoon from the city."

"Stay where you are," she ordered. "And you stay a good ten feet from me at all times."

He grinned, nodding. "Right. I certainly don't want to make this difficult for you. Tell you what, why don't you come over here by the fire and I'll go over there and put a late dinner together. Are you hungry?"

"Yes," she said, annoyed at herself for admitting the truth instead of denying the fact she was literally starving.

He clapped his hands together. "Good. We'll have Thanksgiving early this year."

She walked stiffly over to the fire. "I hope you're not going to cook a turkey." She fell in a heap in front of the hearth, not even glancing at him when he passed by her.

Her feet were shriveled and red when she put them in front of the flames and began wiggling her toes. She gazed into the fire and rubbed her eyes. She yawned, then gave her head a quick little shake. She didn't want to get too relaxed, too comfortable.

"Do you like Mexican casseroles?" he called over.

"Anything's fine," she answered back. At this point she could eat a raw oyster, something she'd never been able to do.

"Good, it doesn't take long to throw one of those together. Then I can come over and join you while it bakes." As he talked he ripped open a package of tortilla chips. He suddenly laughed. "I don't mind doing most of the cooking now because I'm trying to impress you with my skills, but when our relationship becomes more permanent I'll share the kitchen with you."

She glared fixedly at him. "When our relationship becomes more permanent you'll be so old it won't matter who cooks or what is cooked. By then you'll probably be getting your feedings through a tube."

He chuckled. "You know, Blair darling, it's your optimism that first caught my attention; the way you're able to look out into a storm and see only blue skies and sunshine."

She jumped to her feet and asked, "Do you have an inside bathroom?"

He nodded and pointed with a fork to a door in the corner of the room past the beds. "You will find all the latest conveniences behind that door, and if you want to shower and change clothes, you can find some sweat suits in that bottom dresser drawer, and some fleece-lined houseshoes in that closet. I'll have you a drink when you come out. What would you like?"

She moved across the room and opened the drawer, taking out a dark green sweat suit. As she moved to the closet, she glanced over at him, saying, "Rum and Coke."

He grinned and nodded. "You got it."

She felt his eyes follow her into the bathroom, and when she closed the door and noticed there was no lock, she felt a sudden apprehension. Surely he would not invade her privacy. Surely not. Still, she would shower quickly before some evil little thought nibbled at what mind he had—and that certainly wasn't much.

She adjusted the water, stripped quickly, and stepped inside the shower stall. Swiftly she lathered from face to toes and was about to step under the stream to rinse when she heard the door open. "Get out of here!" she yelled through the curtain before he could speak.

"Blair," he said softly, "I have a legal question for you."

"What are you doing in here!" she screeched in alarm.

"Like I said, I have a legal question."

"Well, ask it, then get out!"

He inhaled deeply. "If," he said lightly, "and this

is hypothetical, but if one goes to the trouble of robbing a safe, would it be reasonable to expect that burglar to take only a dollar, or would that burglar be more inclined to clean out the safe? And would the penalty be the same?"

She shook her head in wild disbelief. "You *are* crazy."

"But I need to know, really. A lot depends on the answer."

"Of course the penalty wouldn't be the same. Stealing a dollar is a misdemeanor, but taking everything would most likely result in a felony. Breaking and entering would be the same regardless. But why do you want to know?"

He chuckled. "Because I am about to become a felon. I am going to clean out the safe."

Lathered to the hilt, her mouth fell open. In that instant he pulled the curtain back and stood there as naked as the moment of his entrance into this world. She gave a quick glance for just a fraction of a second and immediately felt a shortness of breath.

He smiled and said politely, "Would you mind moving over just a bit. Don't pay any attention to me, just pretend we're in Japan."

She slapped him across the chest with the wet washcloth. "You better not, Mitch!"

He lowered twinkling blue eyes to hers and she looked downward, only to quickly jerk her head away to face the tile wall, so flustered she could not speak. It was obvious he had not suffered any physical misfortune, he was so perfectly built, so magnificent.

She turned her back to him and started rinsing.

Reaching over, he wrapped his arms around her waist in a firm grasp of possessiveness. The water streamed over her face and down her body, striking his arms and rolling away.

His lips worked through her wet hair and hungrily attacked the back of her neck as his body curved against hers. Slowly she turned in his arms and looked directly into his eyes. "Mitch, didn't anyone ever teach you what beds are for?"

His face lit with a wide grin. "Yes," he whispered, "beds are for—later."

She noticed a single drop of water on long lashes as they stood embracing, the satiny slipperiness of his skin against hers causing her knees to tremble. She wanted to pull away from him, but she simply couldn't manage; her reserves weren't that plentiful. She wanted him—she always had. And it was time to stop fighting it.

The water traveled steadily down her shoulders and back over the curves of her hips, and if it had been boiling, she could not have felt any warmer. She smiled and chided in a whisper, "Some quarantine."

He gave her a firm squeeze and a sweeping kiss at her hairline. "Quarantines are for prevention, learned counsel, and what ails me can't be prevented —only cured. And only then after thorough research, which begins like this. . . ." His lips covered hers in a deep warm kiss.

Slowly her hands went around his neck and she stretched up on her tiptoes, pressing her body gently to his. Very swiftly he kissed her over and over, bodies swaying under the pouring water from the showerhead. There was nothing between them now except a rising passion that they both shared.

Her breasts, soft and full, strained against his chest, as if they were going to burst from sheer longing to be touched. His mouth slipped along her neck, across to her shoulders, into the hollow separating her breasts, and when finally his lips sought out one hardened pink tip, she gasped. Soft foreign mutterings came from her throat, thick sounds of desire.

His arms took her hips as his mouth, his tongue, played along her stomach in sweeping kisses, touching flicks of the tongue stirring a desire so keen and sharp she found herself trembling violently.

Her fingers wound into his hair and she brought him to eye level, where they stood gazing in wonder at each other. Without a word he drew back the curtain and swept her from the shower, leaving the water running. In a fragment of time he held her in wet arms on the bed where the erratic flame of passion lowered, then rose to a new brightness.

Her hands were free, free to roam, to touch—strong, sure hands that had never before belonged to her, but were now hers, hot hands that made him weak, that made him groan, that made him frenzied with an eagerness beyond his control. He crushed her beneath him, then exerted all his strength to be tender.

She struggled strong against him, wanting his masculine power, not his tenderness. Together they flung themselves into an insistent passionate state near violent in intensity. Gasping feverishly, they climbed to a new height where everything that existed was below them. The entire earth floated beneath them while they rushed upward, no more than two feathers carried away by a single soft breeze.

Then the breeze stopped in an overwhelming stillness and they fell off, two feathers drifting back to earth again, leaving behind soft cries hanging at the height.

She lay motionless in his arms, moistening her dry mouth, circling her lips with her tongue. She stretched and sighed. Her eyes glistened for a while, then dulled. "You do realize, Mitch, that this is impossible." Her fingers played in the crisp hair at the back of his neck. "It will never work, not in a million years."

He raised up on his left elbow, his eyes soft, intent on her face. "You won't tell my body, will you? It is definitely under the impression that it works already." He smiled faintly. "Why do I feel that you're mine, Blair? No matter what happens, you always will be. And that's strange because there have been times in these past few years when I really believed I would never want a lasting involvement with any woman, not ever again. But I do. With you, I do."

"Mitch," she said firmly. "It's much too soon to use the word *lasting*. It hasn't been that long ago when you were furious with me. It isn't reasonable to believe you've lost all that anger. Have you?"

He bent his head to hers, brushing her lips with a soft sweep of his mouth.

"Yes, I have. This past week I couldn't think of what I'd lost; all I could think of was what I'd found. And, I assure you, I've found much more than I lost."

Her gaze went past him up to the heavy wooden

beams across the ceiling. Her fingers softly caressed the smooth muscular shoulders, the wet skin of his back. "We didn't dry off," she breathed in a faraway whisper. "And now the bed is damp." She shifted and her breasts nestled against his chest, touching nipple to nipple. With that touch she could feel the firm, solid beating of his heart flowing into her.

The room was lit by a flickering light from the brightly burning fire. A delicious aroma diffused over from the oven and filled the air surrounding them. Her loose blond curls glistened in the glowing light, her blue-green irises sparkled with a hidden smile, her cheeks flushed from a new excitement rising in her.

His eyes devoured her. His hands, his long fingers unconsciously traveled slowly up and down her smooth satiny skin. There was a deep silence for several moments as eyes locked and bodies touched, hands exploring gently. He smiled as his fingers wound in the soft silken curls near her face and said in soft words, almost inaudibly, "I suppose dinner is ready."

With a murmur she slid her arms around him, her fingers spreading on his broad back. "Smells good, doesn't it?"

He touched his lips to hers and breathed, "Uh—hummm. I'm a good cook."

Her mouth parted and burned hungrily against his. Then she relaxed and teased, "Ready to get up and set the table?"

He smiled into half-closed eyes. "How will I ever impress you if you keep avoiding my cooking?"

She looked up at him with a sly grin and touched

her upper lip with the tip of her tongue. "Why don't you give it some thought," she chided in a suggestive whisper. "Women differ from men in that respect. My darling chef, there are different ways to reach our hearts." Her fingers fastened on his face, drawing his mouth back to hers.

Mouths met hard and hungry. There were no more words, no holding back. Possessive, demanding needs consumed them as her body writhed beneath his, moving toward the summit of fulfillment. Joyously they surged together, not aware that at the height of their passion a burning other than their own began to fill the air.

Clinging to each other, giving in to the inner fury seeking release, they blended together as one; one heart, one body, one love. One love consuming, joining two bodies as one for a fleeting eternity. One body taking all, giving all. One heart rocketing them to the summit where they existed together for a flaming beat of time, then burst apart, tumbling down as two again, but holding tightly to each other in a fiery embrace, which at last relaxed and softened until they lay breathless, cradled in each other's arms.

She gave a deep, contented sigh, eyes closed, feeling the fading tremblings of his long, slender body against hers.

He shifted to his back and pulled her into the circle of his arms where he enclosed her gently, her head on his chest, his chin resting on the silky curls. "Do you still dislike the mountains?" he asked softly, kissing the top of her head.

She laughed. "I suppose I'm becoming more receptive to heights. You know, I'm very glad you kidnapped me. It's certainly made my weekend more interesting."

"Oh, the kidnapping was nothing, a snap of the fingers. It was the other crime that seems like the miracle. You've been so opposed to me." He sighed. "Why?"

"Not to you, Mitch, but to the situation, the circumstances. Our setting is not ideal, and I'm sure our feelings for each other will be tested in the coming days. It's not that I didn't feel an attraction to you. I did, from the beginning. I just know that it isn't smart to give in to our feelings this way. We don't know each other."

He gave a short laugh. "Don't you have a complete file on me?"

She rolled her eyes up to his face. "Are you telling me what I have in that file is the truth, that you deserted your wife for another woman? Is that what I'm supposed to believe, to know about you?"

He wrinkled his nose. "Do you smell that?" he asked abruptly as his arms dropped away from her. "Our dinner's burned up!"

Her eyes carried a look of disappointment when he moved from the bed and went directly over to the kitchen, opened the oven, and called out with a laugh, "So much for the Mexican casserole."

Her eyes held him, but she did not laugh. She did not smile. She merely stared at him with a questioning expression on her face.

Minutes later when they sat in front of the fire she would no longer meet his eyes. She slowly chewed the ham on rye he had substituted in place of the charred casserole. Abruptly she dropped the half-

113

eaten sandwich onto the plate and raised the cup of coffee and emptied it with several short swallows, holding the cup between drinks close to her mouth with both hands.

"I'm sorry," he said softly, staring at her intently. "Was it that bad?"

She looked at him briefly, uncertainty in her eyes. "No, of course not."

A frown crossed his face. "Well, what is it then?"

The question hung in the air a long time before she said vaguely, "It's late and I'm tired, I'm going to bed." She started up from the cushion on the floor.

Reaching out, he caught her arm with a firm grip, holding her down. "Wait a minute, Blair," he said in a hoarse voice just above a whisper. "Would you mind letting me in on what's going on inside your head? I'm not stupid; I see the change. I feel it in the air. What is this?"

"Mitch," she said strongly, freeing her arm from his tight fingers, "I am not an expert on everything, but I do know when an issue is being evaded. Many times I advise my clients to skirt those issues that would be self-incriminating." She rose swiftly to her feet. "Thank you for the sandwich and the coffee."

He rose with her, his jaw tightening. "But you're not my attorney, Blair." His eyes were growing more somber. "Or my judge." He cocked his head slightly and asked, "Are you?"

She silently eyed him another long moment, then said softly, "I want to end this discussion."

With a strong shake of his head, he shot back quickly, "No, you don't. You want me to either admit or deny the charge and I'm not going to, simply because it would not solve anything if I did." He gestured with both hands at her. "If I say, 'Yes, I left with another woman,' what would your reaction be?"

She sighed. "I don't want to discuss it, Mitch."

Ignoring her, he went on, "Or if I say, 'No, it's a lie, I was never unfaithful to my wife,' would you, could you believe that?"

"I said I don't want to discuss it, Mitch."

He looked distractedly into the fire, then back to her. "Your attitude is implying guilt, Blair. You're accusing me with your voice, the expression on your face, the way you're looking at me. You think I'm guilty as hell, don't you?" he asked sternly.

"How many times must I say I don't want to discuss it, Mitch?" she answered stiffly. "It's just a shame we had to meet on a legal battleground." She tilted her chin. "Now, please excuse me. I am going to bed." Giving a deep sigh, she turned and walked over to the bed, where she mechanically pulled back the covers.

"But, Blair," he called crisply after her, "we aren't on any legal battleground. You and I have no quarrel. What happens in the court is between Charlotte and me, not you and me."

Standing at the side of the bed, she studied his handsome face intently. "If you believe that, Mitch, then you're much too naive to be a grown man."

"And you are the all-knowing woman, aren't you?" he responded immediately, his voice suddenly harsh. His lips twisted. "You don't want to know about my marriage because it would pose a conflict of interest, it would make you less than the ethical person you think yourself to be in the eyes of the law. It isn't violating any interest or ethics to sleep with me, just don't let it go beyond the physical arena."

She dashed back to the foot of the bed, firmly planting both hands on her hips, her neck stretching like a swan's in his direction. "Did I want to come up here with you? Did I want to have a physical relationship with you? Haven't I fought it from the first time you put your hands on me?" Her eyes blazed at him as she gave her head quick little shakes, lowering her angry voice. "But no, no, pig-headed you! You couldn't accept a sensible rejection; you couldn't accept that it was the best thing for *both* of us. No, you had to impress me with your manliness!" Her eyes flared round. "Well, I'm impressed!" she yelled out.

His eyes had not moved from her face. Slowly he inhaled a long breath, giving her the oddest smile. "Are you?" he asked softly.

She saw the new glint spring to life in the pale irises. His dark hair glistened in the glow of the blazing fire behind him. Standing only in his trousers, his slender muscular frame was outlined by the golden glow from the blazing logs. Her hands unconsciously reached for the knitted band of the sweat shirt and yanked it well over her hips. "I'm going to bed," she said tersely, then added, "alone."

She turned and walked back to the side where she had turned the covers back. Giving him one fleeting I-dare-you glare, she crawled onto the bed, still fully clothed in the oversize sweat suit.

"You expect me to sleep on that wet bed?" he exclaimed in a surprised grunt.

She nestled her head comfortably on the pillow and pulled the sheet and blanket snugly around her neck. "I expect that's your problem," she replied curtly. "There's always the sofa, or the floor, whichever suits you best." She lay on her side, facing his direction, her expression one of watchful distrust.

He gave a single nod and muttered, "All right." He raised his arms, unbuttoned his pants, and let them drop to the floor. He stepped out and kicked the crumpled trousers all the way into the kitchen. Then he paraded naked to the wet bed, jerked back the covers, and fell onto the damp sheet, stretching out full length. He lay glaring up at the ceiling. "You know," he said with a husky sigh, "this is not half-bad."

She smiled. "I'm glad."

"Reminds me of when I used to lie in my crib in a wet diaper."

"My, don't you have an excellent memory," she chided with a soft laugh.

His head turned and he stared at her face. "Of course, I never had to lie in that state for very long; someone always took pity on me."

"I love stories with happy endings," she murmured softly. "I wish there was someone like that here now." Her voice dropped to a whisper. "But there isn't."

His large blue eyes held hers, his brows raised. "Are you telling me you would be cruel to babies, you would allow a baby to lie in a wet diaper?"

"Yes," she replied mockingly soft. "Especially a thirty-two-year-old baby. If *you* had stayed out of *my* shower then you wouldn't be in your present

117

predicament, and your bed would be as dry as mine, and as warm, and as cozy." She winked at him. "Good night and pleasant dreams."

He suddenly jumped from the bed, inhaling a deep breath. "Well, I tried, but it's back to my life of crime." Taking one step, he reached for her covers and ripped them off her with one smooth jerk.

Curled in the sweat suit, she looked up at him with a mockingly innocent expression. "Do you know the penalty that goes with what you are anticipating at this moment?"

"I hope so," he laughed, reaching for her. "But why don't you run it by me one more time, just for the record." Slowly he reached for the shirt and began to undress her, his fingers gently touching her flesh as he drew it over her head.

"Life imprisonment is the least you'll come away with," she whispered, pressing her open hands against his chest.

His warm hands slid the soft cotton pants over her hips and down her legs. "I don't want the least, I want the most, the ultimate." His hands came slowly back up her legs, now naked, trembling from the sensations of his touch.

His eyes swept over her full breasts, lingering a moment, then slowly traveling down the length of her. The sheer warmth from glinting irises made her flinch and hurried her heart into a pronounced new rhythm, like the beat of war drums. She knew this would have to end eventually, but not tonight. Tonight there was no power that could pull her away from him, no power that could hold back the thrill of the moment she experienced moving into his arms, reaching up with her own, and, with a murmur, catching his hungry mouth with hers in a kiss so intense with demand she gasped for breath.

Almost immediately the fire between them blazed beyond control. The strength of his arms, the pressure of his heated body pressing her belly set loose a million new sensations. Her passion matched his, then surpassed his for a prolonged moment as her lips, her hands caressed him in a bold exploration that set him moaning.

Gently he turned her to her back and his lips wandered intimately, searching each and every sensitive area, heightening the ache, prolonging the ecstasy until the need for his inner touch was greater than any need she had ever felt before.

"Mitch," she murmured urgently. "Mitch." Her hands wildly stroked his back and shoulders, then tightened on his flesh to draw him closer to her. "Mitch," she groaned, only to have the single word silenced by his mouth engulfing hers. She felt his tongue join with hers, drawing new tremors of awakening from the deep well of passion.

Bodies joined and the force binding them together reached out and shook the stars free from the heavens. His body consumed hers as the stars fell all around them with a brilliant nearly blinding light. One crushing embrace and her arms clung to him desperately as they journeyed together in a beautiful, breathtaking fall. She gasped out loud in amazement, so real was the tumble.

In the next split-second her trembling body touched something cold and hard and she cried out, "What—"

"It's all right, darling," he gasped between uneven breaths. "The bed broke, that's all." He moved, then lay beside her on an incline.

She looked up at him, a surprised smile spreading along her lips. She laughed, soft, broken laughter erupting between warm quick breaths.

He pulled her up to him, clasping her across his chest. "What's so funny?" he muttered, pressing his smiling mouth to hers. He held her lips a long moment and when he freed her, she burst out laughing. The smile remained fixed on his lips, but the blue eyes laughed with her.

She bit the back of her hand, trying to halt the throaty bubbles of delight shaking her entire frame. Her eyes sparkled at him. "Mitch, do you realize"— her face crinkled with laughter—"in a few short hours what we've done?" She lifted a limp hand. "The bath's a mess, that bed's wet, this bed's broken, the dinner burned up . . ." She choked out, "You'll be lucky if the cabin's still standing in another twenty-four hours."

He laughed. "I've been here many, many times and nothing like this has ever happened before. But, then, I never came in holding a two-legged curly-haired tornado in my arms."

She turned her head and pressed her mouth to his chest.

"I love you, Blair," he whispered, his fingers moving slowly through her hair. "I love you very much."

Closing her eyes, she bit her lip to keep back the tempting words he wanted to hear, the words she wanted to say. She lay silent, unmoving, feeling his hand twisting her hair. Suddenly a shudder went through her and after a long moment she whispered, "Mitch, where are we going to sleep?"

His hand slid from her hair along her neck and down her smooth shoulders before he sighed. "I'll get dry bed linens for the other bed. Are you sleepy?"

"Yes," she breathed. "Very."

But she was still awake, craddled in his arms while he slept when the sun broke through the dark in the early morning hours. Her eyes caressed him while he lay sleeping, memorizing each beautiful feature of his face, the bronzed smoothness of his skin, the sleek relaxed muscular body.

The fire had burned low; only a few remaining coals lay smoldering on the hearth. She simply did not know what she would do in the days ahead.

CHAPTER EIGHT

It was late morning when she awoke and found herself alone in the bed. A new fire was burning in the hearth, but as she lay peeking sleepily through the sunlit windows, she knew once the chill was removed from the room there would be no further need for a fire.

Yawning wide, she raised up from the pillow and gazed around the room. There was no sign of Mitch. Her mouth parted with surprise and her head jerked around to the bathroom door which was ajar, the room dark. Sitting up in the middle of the bed, she craned her neck to look out the window for sight of him. Realizing the car was gone, her lips pursed thoughtfully as she crawled out of bed and went into the bathroom. She showered quickly and pulled on his oversize robe that hung on the back of the bathroom door. Finding the fabric damp, she realized he must have showered while she slept so soundly she had not known when he left the bed or even when he drove off in the car.

Wondering where he had gone, she walked back into the living room and looked over to the brass bed with one side of its mattress settled on the floor. A romantic smile touched her lips as she quickly made up the bed she had just vacated. Then she walked toward the cabinet and the delicious smell of fresh perked coffee. She poured a cup, then stood looking out the window above the sink. It was a serene May morning, the beautiful spring colors outside reflecting the season. The trees were the greenest greens and brightly colored wildflowers flamed up from the low bushes and vines.

Raising the cup to her lips, she realized she was happy, perhaps happier than she had ever felt before. This was her first truly rapturous love affair, one in which she had lost herself completely to pleasure-seeking sensations of the body. It was a strange feeling, one of being lost and found at the same time. And as long as she didn't think of tomorrow, she could be content with today.

With the coffee cup in her hand she went back into the bathroom, placed the cup on the counter, and briefly examined her face in the square mirror above the lavatory. Quite obviously she needed some work. The natural blush was gone from her cheeks, replaced by a pale ivory sheen. Deep blue-green eyes peering back at her from the mirror looked larger and darker than normal. At least nothing appeared wrong with her lips except they seemed fuller than usual and perhaps more red. She smiled bleakly.

There was nothing she could do since she had not brought along makeup.

She pulled open a drawer to search for a brush, found one and immediately began separating the fine blond silken curls which were tangled together. When she had the hair brushed loose and falling smoothly at her shoulders, she lowered the brush back toward the drawer and released it with a soft thud. She started to push closed the drawer when her eyes halted on a tube of lipstick in the corner. She stood for a moment staring blindly at the tube. Something about it struck her as strange.

Lifting it up, she held it in front of her eyes. A frenzied beat began to start somewhere deep in her chest. She realized she had a tube exactly like it at home, purchased only last week during a noon shopping spree at Biggers Department Store. The lady behind the cosmetic counter had said it was the latest color, a soft plum labeled Springtime.

She turned the tube so that she could read the label and the word *Springtime* jumped out at her. She froze. This wasn't her lipstick. Whose was it? And how did it get into this drawer? Immediately she knew it didn't belong to his former wife. No, Charlotte wore only bold reds, the deepest reds.

She slung the tube back into the drawer and slammed it closed. "Damn," she breathed angrily, grabbing up the cup and rushing out of the bath. She took a big swallow of coffee and grunted again, "Damn!" She wasn't the only woman who had been in this cabin this week!

She shook her head wildly, exclaming aloud, "No wonder the damned bed fell in. He's worn it out!"

Her angry mind began to receive stabs of lightning. It belonged to Marsha Partlow. She knew it. What would a woman who had been out of the country first do upon arrival back home? Go shopping, of course. She would buy the latest fashions, the latest everything, including lipstick.

She paced the floor, the remaining coffee sloshing against the sides of the cup, her mind scrambling back through the week. She had not heard a single word from Mitch Morgan until he appeared on her doorstep last night. He had not called or dropped by, not a word. Nothing. He had been too busy. Her brows rose, her lips twisted, her head tilted so that her chin almost touched her neck. That's why the refrigerator was so well-stocked. He and Marsha had been eating out of it all week. The evidence certainly was piling fast against him. Overwhelming evidence.

Her chin jutted out and she ground her teeth together. He would not discuss the "other woman." Every time the subject came up he changed the topic. He wouldn't deny it—because he couldn't. The color flooded back to her cheeks and flames of anger began a slow, deliberate war dance in her eyes. He had sounded so convincing when he told her he had found more than he had lost. No doubt of that. He had found more than any six men had lost. She grabbed the top of her head with one hand. She had to think. She had to think clearly. Impatiently she paced. She was too angry to feel the hurt. Her mind went back to her original theory; he was using her in some obscure way to feed his male ego, to strike back at his wife. He was using her because he held her responsible for stripping him of his material possessions. He was using her out of spite.

She sighed heavily, then angrily slammed the cup against the stone fireplace. He was a damned good actor; he had fooled her completely—almost. She had never freed herself totally from the doubt that the charge of the other woman had been true in some context. Now she was sure of it. She clutched her head tightly, letting go a long "Ohhh." She had been such a fool. But she would take care of that. When she finished with him she would probably need a lawyer. Emotional deceit was the worst kind, and for that deceit he was going to pay the full penalty.

At the sound of the car pulling up on the gravel she inhaled several quick deep breaths and prepared herself. She had never been one motivated by spiteful actions, never been one to strike back blindly at someone, but in this particular situation she felt justified.

She took great care in fixing her expression just right for him when the door opened and his smiling self walked in. She smiled sweetly and he flashed white teeth back at her. He had a package under one arm, and was wearing a white cotton jacket over a deep blue shirt with a knitted waistband overlapping faded denims that hugged his lean frame. On his feet were moccasins of soft brown. His eyes were like magnetic blue fields shining brightly, vibrantly alive, accentuated by the smooth tanned skin of his face.

Chuckling, he held the package out to her. "I've been shopping," he said lightly.

She pursed her lips. "Oh, really—on Sunday? What was open?"

He clicked his tongue. "I've got connections. Here, try these on."

With the smile pasted firm on her lips she accepted the package he held out. Slowly she untied the white string and folded back the brown paper. She smiled tightly up at him and sighed. "This is my first CARE package."

He flashed a lop-sided grin and pointed to his chest with one thumb. Mockingly deep, he said, "Stick with me, kid, I'll take care of you."

She glared up at him and for a moment the grin wavered, then came back strong when she replied, "I'll bet you will. I'll just bet you will." She was still considering his joking words when she lifted new denims from the paper, followed by a soft white cotton blouse and a soft white buckskin vest with long leather fringes. At the bottom of the package was a pair of moccasins, size six. "You like white, don't you?" she said, holding up the blouse and vest, one in each hand.

He nodded and laughed. "Yes. The vest is because I didn't know what size bra and it'll serve as kind of a shield if we go out."

She laughed mockingly soft. "Mitch, you're so thoughtful." She dropped the items from her hands and inhaled a deep breath, throwing out her chest, allowing the robe to pull apart, revealing the hollow between her breasts. "What size do you think I am, darling?" she asked suggestively. Large round eyes caught his face.

His mouth parted slightly in amusement, then closed as he swallowed. "I don't know," he gestured with a quick movement of one hand. "But I would say you're certainly well-developed and healthy."

Her seductive grin spread as her hands touched the front of the robe, pressing in lightly. "Oh, come on, Mitch, make a guess."

He stepped toward her, his tongue brushing his lips, his eyes frozen on the opening. Seeing the sudden brightness in his irises, she adjusted the robe and leaned forward to try on the moccasins, sighing a soft laugh. "You failed, and that surprises me. For a man who spends so much time measuring sheetrock I would have thought it would have been a snap."

She pulled on the right shoe as he said, "There's a big difference between measuring sheetrock and breasts. I've yet to receive an order for sheetrock cut to fill a bra."

She laughed with delight. "Oh, Mitch, you do have such a sense of humor." She pulled her leg up and the robe gapped open, exposing her thigh. She twisted her foot at him. "Perfect fit. Absolutely amazing, isn't it?"

His eyes were not on her foot or the new moccasins. Slowly he lowered himself to his knees beside her, his mouth open. "Uh-huh."

When he reached for her, she quickly jumped to her feet and clapped her hands. "I love them, Mitch." She turned a time or two, doing a little dance in the new shoes, and with each sweeping move the robe billowed open slightly.

He sat down flat on the floor and looked up at her, his eyes wide, filled with a passionate expression. "Come here, Blair," he whispered huskily, extending one arm toward her.

128

She waltzed over and swooped down for the other garments. "I've got to dress. I can't wait to try everything on. I'll be right back."

She hastened into the bathroom and shut the door, where she put any quick-change artist to shame. Within two seconds she was dressed. Walking back into the room, she found him still sitting on the floor.

Looking up at her when she entered, he asked, "What happened to the cup?" He pointed to the shattered remains.

She made a little grimace. "I dropped it," she said softly, trying to put the smile back on her lips.

He cradled his knees and said, "You dropped it against the fireplace? That's kind of hard to do, isn't it? Looks to me like you threw it."

She stood facing him. Slowly her hands ran down the side of the new clothes. "Why would I do that, Mitch?" she inquired softly.

"I don't know. But you did, didn't you?" he said, his chin resting on his knees. "What is it, Blair? You're not exactly acting like yourself."

She stood frozen a moment. "If you're upset about the cup, I'll be more than happy to replace it," she finally answered, twisting one leather fringe around her finger. "I didn't realize you had a sentimental attachment to it, but obviously you do."

"I don't have a sentimental attachment to the damned cup, Blair." He rose slowly to his feet. "But I feel a strong attachment to you." He squared his shoulders and cocked his head. "When I left here you were asleep. I come back, and what do I find, some modern-day Jezebel, flaunting herself all over the place. You don't have to play those kinds of games with me, not to turn me on to you. All you have to do is look at me. Why are you looking away from me now? Huh? Why did you slam the cup against the stone? What happened while I was gone? Did you have a nightmare or something? Is that it?" His inquisitive eyes filled with concern. "Tell me, will you?"

She lifted her shoulders and her hand dropped from the leather vest. Slowly she met his probing gaze. "You might say I experienced something of a nightmare. But it's not important," she concluded in a whisper. "As for playing games, monkey see, monkey do. I'm sure you've heard that old saying, haven't you?"

He brushed back a fallen strand of hair with his forearm and held the back of his hand against his head. "If that is supposed to make any kind of sense to me, I assure you it doesn't. Are you accusing me of playing some kind of game? Is that what you're doing?" He looked her in the face and quietly said, "If you are, you're wrong." He pointed to his chest with one finger, adding, "This monkey ain't playing no game."

Turning, she gave her head one little shake, then dropped to her knees and began to pick up the broken glass.

He knelt down beside her and bent to pick up a piece. "I'll help you," he said emotionlessly.

"Why don't you repair your bed, Mitch. I'll clean this up." She gave a short sarcastic laugh. "A man of your virility and strength should never be down to just one bed. Or maybe you should reinforce the ones you have with steel beams, you know like the ones used in skyscrapers."

Without a word he rose to his feet and walked over to the crippled bed. Then he raised his foot and kicked the other side in. At the loud noise Blair jerked her head around in time to see him storm angrily from the house, slamming the door so hard the hinges vibrated. She had not thought of arousing such hostility in him, had not intended to make him so angry. But now that she had, she didn't regret it.

She was at the garbage can, placing the broken cup inside when he rushed back inside, glared over to her from the door, and said in a harsh, controlled voice, "I don't need this, not from you, not from any woman. If you want to tell me what's the basis for this radical change in your attitude, I'll listen, but if you can't talk to me, then maybe I'd just better drive you home."

She nodded in agreement and said coolly, "Yes, I think you'd better. I'll get my things."

It didn't surprise her in the least when he slammed out again.

Not a word passed between them all the way down the mountain. She refused to look at him, and the times she felt his questioning eyes on her she looked out her side window. She felt haggard, washed-out. She felt he had made a complete fool of her, and with that thought came a piercing pain. She knew she would be a long time forgetting this encounter, if ever.

When he pulled onto the interstate, she glanced at her watch. He inquired calmly. "Am I not traveling fast enough for you? Would you like for me to break the speed limit?"

She ignored his question. "Blair!" he demanded harshly. "Damn it, give me a break. At least tell me what I'm accused of. I don't have the foggiest idea of what happened. Is that asking too much?"

Her gaze wandered over to him briefly, then away. His drawn face provided the image of someone totally in the dark. He was an excellent actor. She would have to give him that much credit. He was playing the role of the innocent victim right down to the last word. For the first time, the fleeting doubt that she might be mistaken crossed her mind, but she shook it away. No, she had examined the lipstick carefully. Perhaps the evidence was only circumstantial, but it was enough for her. "Mitch," she said in a low monotone, "whatever was between us is over. I want you to understand that clearly. It's over. I don't want you coming to my home again. I don't want you bothering me in any way, not ever again."

He glared at her intensely for a moment, then shook his head one time, declaring under his breath more to himself than to her, "This should prove it once and for all; all women are crazy as ten-legged spiders. This should do you, Mitch boy, for a long, long time." Then he lapsed into a heavy silence.

As soon as he pulled into her drive she saw the front door of her house standing ajar. Her mouth twitched with disbelief before she spluttered accusingly, "You—you didn't close my door."

He immediately jerked the car to a halt. "Yes, I did," he replied emphatically.

The door on her side bolted open and she jumped

132

out. "Well, you didn't close it good. If you had, it wouldn't be standing wide open, now would it? I probably don't have a thing left inside," she said shakily, slamming the car door.

He sat slumped behind the steering wheel, shaking his head slowly from side to side. Then he got out and followed her, saying in an even tone, "Why don't you wait for me?"

At the doorway she paused for a deep breath, then went inside. She stood looking down at the mess of torn books in the living room when he walked up behind her. Pages were strewn everywhere, the covers chewed and gnawed beyond recognition.

His hands came up to her shoulders and he said softly, "That dog next door must have pushed the door open. I never knew of a burglar taking the time to eat up books."

She shook free of his hands, moving a step forward, her head bowed, her eyes suddenly filled with hot tears. "My damned books," she choked between sobs. "She ate every one of them." Her hands came up and she angrily wiped at her tears. "And it's your fault."

"I'm sorry, Blair," he muttered an apology. "I'll replace the books. I'll make it right."

She spun around and cried out, "As if you could! As if you could make anything right! Why don't you just get out! That's the only right thing you can do for me!"

His lips twisted as he said grimly, "I'm going to check the rest of your house, and then I will. And don't you worry, you won't be bothered with me

133

again." He turned on his heel and heavy steps took him down the hall.

A moment of silence and he called back grudgingly, "Something tells me that dog next door is a helluva lot smarter than I am." Angry steps brought him back into the living room. "Everything's okay in the rest of the house," he grunted and stormed out the door, calling back, "I'll get your things out of the car."

While he was outside she began to pick up the torn pages from the living room carpet. Almost at once he was back. Walking into the living room, he slung her clothing into the chair. "Your yesterday's wardrobe," he said flatly.

She jumped to her feet quickly and said in a huff, "If you'll wait a minute, you can have these back." She ripped the vest off and tossed it at him. "I'm sure you'll find someone else who can put them to use tromping up and down mountains with you!"

"You keep it," he returned, slinging it back into her arms. "It might make the next one as crazy as it made you!" he threw out cynically. He started moving fast to the door, then halted and said back over his shoulder, "I just remembered something else," he said dryly. "I found your lipstick on the bathroom floor this morning. As a matter of fact I nearly broke my neck on it when I stepped out of the shower."

She froze and her eyes blazed.

He went on sarcastically. "No doubt, a booby trap."

He took a step and she stopped him with the angry words, "What did you say!" She stared at him open-mouthed.

He returned her stare in confusion. "It's no big deal, Blair. I'll get it back to you. It's only a tube of lipstick." He paused. "Were you a deprived child or something? You really get excited over your possessions."

Dropping the gathered papers back onto the floor, her eyes widened and her voice rose close to a scream. "I didn't have any lipstick!"

"Counsellor," he said in a placid tone, "I have been accused of everything except that; I don't wear lipstick." He leaned toward her and lowered his voice. "But I might start. After this weekend I might just start. But rest assured, I won't use yours, I'll buy my own tube." His hand reached for the doorknob.

"What I'm telling you," she all but screeched, "is that the tube you found does *not* belong to me! And I'll go one step further—it doesn't belong to Charlotte either. It isn't Charlotte's and it isn't mine. Can you absorb that through your thick skull?"

With growing confusion he shook his head. Glancing sideways at her face thoughtfully, he finally ventured, "I suppose it's possible that it isn't." He nodded and half-whispered, "I suppose it could be Marsha's."

Her system simply could not absorb any more shocks. Her arms dropped limp at her sides. Not even surprise could mask her face now. He had admitted it plain out in the clearest terms possible. "Good-bye, Mitch," she whispered following a long moment of silence.

He looked at her with bewilderment, then walked out without a word.

She was so taken aback by his admission, all she

could do was collapse on the sofa, dazed and confused. It didn't make any sense. Each time the other woman's name had cropped up in conversation he had turned mute—then he stands in her doorway and proclaims the truth.

She felt desperate, her mind blunted, her thoughts wild and erratic. He had forced his way into her life and put some kind of spell on her, to ruin her. And so he had. She felt absolutely destroyed; slayed by his touch, annihilated by his passion, struck down by her own wanton desires. Her good senses had told her from the beginning to resist him, but she had not followed her good senses. He wanted her—he had her. And it had all been so easy. It had taken her twenty-nine years to get this stupid. If an Olympics were held for stupidity, she would come away with the gold medal. She had behaved recklessly, tossing all caution to the winds. Her strongest impulse was to hate him, but somewhere along the line she had lost the ability to even do that well. Somewhere along the line she had done the one thing she knew she should have never done. She had fallen in love with him.

She lay spent, motionless, while an overwhelming emptiness filled her, then spread throughout the house. Darkness had come when she finally roused herself from the sofa. She didn't like to lose, she couldn't accept defeat, not gracefully. And yet her life was filled with defeats—other people's. Mangled marriages, lost loves, torn lives. She had been prepared to help them with their defeats, but who would help her with hers?

Walking down the hall, she heard the telephone

136

ring sharply. The immediate vision of Mitch on the other end froze her. Slowly she turned back and walked to the kitchen extension. She was silent a moment when she lifted the receiver, then said a low, "Hello."

"Blair?" Wayne Fairfield spoke quietly. "I have been trying to reach you since last night. I even came back over this morning to talk with you, but you weren't home. I stuck my head inside your front door and called you, but you didn't answer. You weren't home, were you?"

"No, Wayne, I wasn't."

He sighed. "Good. When I saw your car in the drive I thought maybe you just didn't want to answer me." He cleared his throat nervously. "I really would like to talk with you about what happened last evening. Would it be all right if I came over?"

"Not tonight, Wayne," she responded quickly. "I'm really very tired."

"I hate to insist, Blair," he went on softly, "but I really feel the need to clear the air between us. I'm afraid I behaved badly and I would like to make amends. I'll drop by and get a pizza if you haven't eaten, and we can talk over that and coffee."

She looked at her watch. Eight o'clock. She sighed. "Just for a little while, Wayne."

When she replaced the receiver, she wondered why she had submitted to his request. Inhaling deeply, she went into the hallway where the thought struck that it had been Wayne, not Mitch, who left the front door ajar. It gave her an odd feeling to know she had wrongfully accused Mitch. That

137

wasn't the kind of mistake she made on a regular basis.

Brushing her hair back with her hand, she made up her mind she would apologize to him if she ever saw him again. That possibility seemed very unlikely, but it might happen someday. The city wasn't so large that an accidental meeting wouldn't take place. Remote, but a possibility.

She walked into the bathroom and turned on the lights. She stripped off the clothes he had bought her and took a bath, soaking in the tub for several minutes, allowing the warm water to soak into her pores and wash away some of the anxiety she felt. The unwelcomed thought of the two of them in the shower only last night brought her up out of the water to stand under the shower and rinse quickly. Stepping out, she dried thoroughly, then went into the dressing room where she slipped an ivory-colored caftan over her head. She adjusted the long sleeves and fixed the sash, then applied light touches of makeup to her pale skin. Finally she reached down to the brass lipstick holder, her eyes following her hand. She decided against using the tube of Springtime glaring back at her. As a matter of fact, she lifted the tube from the holder and dropped it into the wastepaper basket. She would never use it again, and didn't want it around as a reminder of what a fool she'd been.

She clutched the sides of her head, trying to get past the barrier of her own thoughts. How could she allow herself to be such a fool? Not exploring beyond what appeared to be? He had as much as admitted she had been the second woman in that cabin with him this week. The woman named Marsha had been there sometime earlier. Mitch had actually, at long last, admitted as much.

On thinking back, she realized Charlotte Morgan had presented a black picture of her marriage to Mitch. A picture she had believed, just as she was inclined to believe all her clients. Meeting Mitch had not altered that picture. He had approached her in anger and she had met that approach with suspicion. Well-based suspicion as it now turned out.

Her thoughts broke off at the sound of the doorbell. When she answered the ring, Wayne came inside carrying the pizza, a sheepish grin on his face. "Peace," he said, holding the box out to her.

"I haven't put on the coffee," she said, taking the box and leading the way into the kitchen. "I'll do it now." She placed the box on the table and went over to the sink.

"You look very nice," he said as he seated himself, his hazel eyes running over her. "Nice, indeed," he added softly.

She peered around at him with a hint of a smile. "Thank you."

When she walked over to the table to join him, he sat nodding his head, an unusual gleam in his eyes. "You know, Blair"—leaning back in the chair, he stared directly into her eyes—"I think maybe I misinterpreted the kind of relationship you wanted, or needed. I've been kind of a fool."

She frowned and immediately switched the conversation. "Are you hungry?" she questioned, reaching over to the box on the table.

He caught her hand in mid-air. "You do know

what I'm talking about, don't you?" He squeezed her fingers.

She gave a low, uneasy little laugh. "I hope not," she said, trying to maintain a lightness in her words.

Holding her hand firmly he went on. "I must be the world's biggest idiot. All this time I thought you wanted this platonic farce, and while I've been Virginia's perfect gentleman you've been carrying on behind my back." He shrugged. "I take you out in public to respectable places and then when I bring you home you've got some married guy stashed away inside."

She wrenched her hand free from his and said hotly, "That is utter nonsense, Wayne. I won't even dignify such a statement with a rebuttal."

He bit into his bottom lip, then released it. "You won't—or can't?" he mocked.

"Don't play words with me," she said, her eyes narrowing furiously. "I'm *not* answering your charge, and I suspect you might need to leave now."

He gave a cynical smile and leaned forward, searching her face. "Pretending is over between us, Blair. I understand what you want now, so there's no reason for you to look elsewhere. I can provide all the excitement you need. I realize I've been a bore with this 'nice guy' routine, but I misread you." He reached out to touch the side of her face.

She withdrew quickly from his approaching hand. "Wayne, get out," she demanded harshly. "Get out of my home and take your damned pizza with you!"

He was startled, a fact obvious by the way his mouth fell open. "What is this?"

"This is an eviction! From my home! From my life! Get out!"

His hand hung in mid-air. "I don't understand," he said abruptly. "If you're worried about your neighbors, I parked around the corner. That's what the others do, isn't it?"

"Then you've got yourself a nice walk back to your car!" She slapped the pizza off her table and the box slid into his lap. Her eyes blazed. "Out! Out! Out!"

He jumped up. "Okay! Okay! I'm going." He looked at her, oddly bewildered. "I—I thought I had it all worked out."

She merely shook her head and ushered him to the door. When she flipped the bolt after his hurried departure, she stood leaning against it, feeling a quick rising pain inside her.

She pressed her head against her arm folded on the door. She was still standing there when she heard the car pull up in the drive. "Oh, no," she groaned aloud. She wouldn't even consider letting him in again. Ignoring the doorbell, she turned and started back to the kitchen.

Then a knock and the single word, "Blair?"

She stopped and turned back. It was Mitch. Hesitantly she opened the door.

He smiled into her solemn face and said lightly, "Wasn't that your friend I passed down the block carrying a pizza?"

"What do you want, Mitch?" she whispered, ignoring his jesting inquiry.

His gaze remained on her face as his hand reached into his jacket and he held the tube of lipstick in front of her eyes. "Do you remember the story about how the war was lost because of the nail?"

She stared blankly at the tube he pressed into her hand.

"Well, do you really want a love to be lost because of this?"

Blair remained silent, not meeting his piercing gaze.

"I want to tell you about the owner of this lipstick," Mitch said gently.

"Marsha Partlow," she whispered.

"Yes, Blair. Marsha Partlow."

CHAPTER NINE

"Mitch," she cried out, "do you realize that you are admitting, that you have admitted she was up there with you?" She flung the lipstick at him, hitting him with a soft thud on the chest.

"Blair," he protested loudly, "I admitted she was up there this week, but not with me. You conjured that up in your own little mind. Marsha Partlow was up there with Ben Partlow, her husband and a vice-president in my corporation. When are you ever going to start considering all the facts instead of swallowing all the bull Charlotte fed you?"

Her expression changed from shock to dismay. "She has a husband . . ." Blair whispered.

"Of course she has a husband. She's had a husband all along, Blair. He was with us in Saudi Arabia."

She began to cry from frustration. "Why didn't you tell me? Why have you allowed me to belie—"

He interrupted harshly, taking a firm hold of her

arm. "Now get this straight, counsellor, I haven't allowed you to believe anything. You have believed what you chose to believe, what was convenient for you to believe. I've spent a good many years of my life playing the jealousy game, denying this and denying that, but I was finished with that game a long time ago. And I'm not going to start playing it with you, Blair. Now, either you learn to trust me and believe what I say to you or we'll say good-bye right now and save ourselves a lot of grief later. Love is trust, Blair. If you love me, then trust me. Charlotte got the insane notion years ago that Marsha and I were in love, having some kind of torrid affair amid the sheetrock. And you know what? It almost cost me my best friend, Ben. But they had a strong marriage. They had to survive Charlotte's lies and innuendos." He looked at her sincerely. "I want you to believe me simply because I'm telling you the truth."

She nodded somewhat reluctantly, saying with a long sigh, "I don't understand it at all, Mitch." She stared at him confused. "Why would you marry a woman like that?"

His fists clenched tightly and he held both motionless in the air in front of him. "Can't you understand? I have been trying to tell you from the beginning. She hasn't always been as she is now. She changed, Blair. People do that—change. Come into the living room and we'll sit down and talk about this. It's something we should have done first, not now. But I suppose now is better than never."

She stood quiet a long moment, not at all sure she needed to know Mitch's version. Finally the attorney in her conceded to the woman. Maybe she didn't

144

need to know, but she had reached the point where she *had* to know.

Mitch sensed the battle going on inside her head. "You're at a real disadvantage here, Blair. We might as well face the fact that your profession has tainted your views of connubial bliss. Every time you go into that courtroom you've divorced a man. Not long ago you divorced me. You've lost your trust in men, Blair. You've hidden yourself from any real involvement by continuing that relationship with Wayne Fairfield. You felt secure with him because he's perfectly willing to play your 'hands-off' game." His brows rose as he lowered himself on the sofa beside her. "I'm not going to play that game with you, as you already know. Now, you made a perfect ass of yourself today over a tube of lipstick, which incidentally happened to belong to another woman. An incident like that could have destroyed a lot of relationships, but in ours it worked to an advantage. It gave us both some insight into your feelings about me. You care, whether or not you're willing to admit it. I know you do."

She clutched her forehead tightly, giving several quick shakes. "I—I don't know." She sat rigidly. "I really don't know what I feel, or what it would matter one way or the other. You do realize that it's far from being over for you. It may be months, maybe years before this mess is resolved."

He turned from her, shaking his head. "I want you to understand one thing, Blair. It is over. Now it's over," he repeated in a whisper. "I spent an entire week of my life weighing my values, deciding what's really important to me. That house isn't important to me, or my car, or the money, not to the extent I would tie up my life in a battle to get it back. I'm free, and I'm going to stay free."

There was a moment of silence. She wasn't sure she understood what he was saying, so she was the first to speak. "I'm sorry, Mitch, but I'm not sure I understand." She stared, dazed, at his profile.

He hesitated, then said in gentle tones, "Butterflies are free, counsellor, and so am I." A strange smile curved his lips. "That divorce decree gave me my wings. I'm free." His shoulders relaxed. "And I intend to stay that way."

She sat speechless, looking at him. "You mean you're not fighting the divorce, you're not going to try to reclaim your possessions?" Her mouth fell slightly open, her eyes filled with surprise.

"That's right." He straightened, caught her shoulders, and gave her a quick kiss on her still parted lips. "You did a good job," he teased. "Not only did you take away most of what I had worked all my life to have, you made me happy it's gone. Now, what man could ask for more than that?" He pulled back and his blue eyes scanned her face. "It's best for all of us, don't you see? Charlotte has what she wants, your good name remains unblemished, and I, I have my freedom. And that means I'm free to love you, and you're free to love me. I don't think I want to jeopardize this arrangement." He laughed confidently. "Do you?"

She couldn't share his laughter; she couldn't even manage a smile. She asked softly, "Have you changed your mind because of me, Mitch?"

His smile slowly vanished. "Partly," he said at

last. "And for me." He gazed steadily into her eyes. "And even for Charlotte. I don't want to embarrass her. I have no idea why she handled it this way because she could have had the divorce years ago. But she always said she would never divorce me." He repeated softly, "I don't know why she went to all the lengths to do what she did. But I'm sure in her own mind she had it all figured out. And that's the only bothersome aspect of this ordeal, Blair. I still have no idea why." The smile came back slowly to his lips. "But I am content with the results."

She surprised herself with the blunt question, "What happened to your marriage, Mitch? When did you stop loving her? What went wrong?" At last she felt unbound by prior commitments, felt she wasn't betraying any confidences to seek the truth. Now she could ask the questions that had haunted her mind since the moment they first met.

He looked at her with a slightly tortured expression on his face. Sounding boyishly wistful, he asked, "Do you suppose we could have something to drink before I begin with those answers?"

"What would you like? Coffee or something stronger?"

"Uh—something stronger."

"I just have wine. Will that do?"

He nodded. "Put mine in a mug."

She looked at him questioningly. "If it's that unpleasant for you to discuss, maybe we shouldn't."

He gave a shake of his head. "No, I think you should be aware of the circumstances." He smiled bleakly. "A regular wineglass will do."

Somewhat annoyed with herself for upsetting him,

she rose and poured the two glasses of white wine. Slowly she returned to the sofa and passed one into his waiting hand. "Really, Mitch, we don't have to go back into the past."

He sighed heavily. "Perhaps one trip back is required, Blair, in order to go forward. I think it's important for you to know that I planned on spending my life with her the day we married." Taking a sip of wine he shrugged, then went on. "She was a beautiful woman, and still is, as you well know, and I was very much in love with her. We were married ten years ago in El Paso, Texas. We're both native Texans. But soon after the wedding I bought the business here and of course we moved. It took several years to make the business solid. That was working from daylight to dark, sometimes earlier, sometimes later. We bought a small house not far from here the first year, then the third year we moved into a much larger, finer house. The business had become successful, I was making a good deal of money, and we were secure financially. At that time I was twenty-five, three years out of college, the owner of my own business and home, and we were saving money, investing some. I wanted to start our family. So did she." He paused and took another long, thoughtful drink. "All our friends and neighbors had children. We had everything going for us, or so we thought." He gave a short, almost bitter laugh. "It's one thing to not want children, Blair, but it's quite another thing to discover that you can never have one, not one of your own."

Her eyes widened and her brows rose. "She couldn't have children?" she interjected in a whisper.

He grimaced and nodded his head. "That's right." He threw out one hand in a quick gesture. "What can I say? It was devastating to both of us."

"Mitch," she murmured, "you don't need to te—"

"Yes," he said emphatically. "I do! You need to know, Blair. You hear only what your clients want to tell you, and sometimes the truth is skirted altogether. The fact that Charlotte could not have a child destroyed us. Our marriage crumbled like it had been made of clay all along. From that point on it was downhill. And a few months later Charlotte had her first affair." He smiled sadly. "The first of many."

She stared speechless at him in a slow devouring numbness. Finally she whispered, "Please, don't say anything more, Mitch. Please."

He looked at her long and hard, his eyes narrowing, his gaze lingering on her face. "I will say it all—this one time."

She choked out, "But—don't you understand, you don't have to."

He obviously misunderstood, for he said harshly, "Oh, but I do. I have to tell you that our marriage ended six years and a dozen men ago." His words deliberately slowed and softened. "But the crazy thing, Blair, is that the more she did, the more insanely jealous she became of me. It was not the other way around, as you might expect. By that time I didn't care anymore. I wanted out. It's incredible what people do to each other for better or for worse. Maybe those words should be stricken from the marriage vows altogether, because when it's for worse it's usually over. And who should know that better than you?"

"Mitch," she cried in alarm, clutching his arm and shaking it, causing the wine to slosh out of his glass. "Stop it. I don't want to hear any more."

He stared at her, uncomprehending. His shoulders slumped and a long silence fell between them.

"I thought you wanted to know," he whispered in a low voice, finally ending the quiet.

She stirred. "I did, Mitch, but I never realized how painful it would be for you. I don't want that." She was trembling.

He smiled at her grimly, studying her face. He reached out and closed his arms around her, whispering against the top of her head. "It's okay. Let's get it behind us now, tonight. You see, for years I've wondered what I could have done differently. Only recently did I realize that there was nothing I could have done."

She pulled away and touched his lips with her fingers. "I am very sorry that she didn't love you when she should have needed your love and when she could have had it all. She needed to love you then, but she didn't, and whatever her reasons, that part of your life is ended. Now it's my time." And looking at him she realized it was her time. She needed him, so much so she felt a physical ache.

Her eyes fixed intently on his face and for the first time she felt peaceful and content about his place in her life. The worrisome thoughts were falling somewhere in the distance, leaving her free to love him. At last she could dismiss the past with all its questions. She didn't have all the answers, but she had all she needed. She wanted his love and nothing more. Reaching out, she gently touched the side of his face. "Mitch," she whispered, drawing closer to him. "It's all behind us now. Let's leave it there. Let's begin anew." Her mouth lifted to his and she softly brushed his lips, then smiled. Slowly her smile faded as she drew back, looking at him.

"Do you mean that?" he asked seriously.

"Of course I do. I never meant anything more in my life." She stared at him, unable to read even a glimpse into his thoughts.

He moistened his lips with his tongue. "Well, if you do, let's do it right. Let's get married."

Her mouth gaped open in surprise. "What?" She gave him a look of total disbelief.

"Let's get married. We'll drive to Washington, catch a flight to Vegas, and this time tomorrow we'll be married." He hesitated briefly. "I love you, Blair, and I don't want anything to come between us, not ever again."

She was stunned speechless. She tried to be light, saying, "Aren't you being somewhat impractical, Mitch?" She laughed nervously, softly. "You've been free such a short while."

He did not smile. Lean, strong fingers closed around hers. "Blair, I have just asked you to marry me. Believe me, I would not be walking out of one hell only to reenter by another gate. If I didn't truly love you, then I would be satisfied with the present arrangement; go on sleeping with you with no promises, no ties. But I care too much about you."

"Let's give it time, Mitch. It isn't fair of you to

expect me to marry you, not now, not this soon. I—I'm sorry, but I need more time."

He gave a sad smile and a single shake of his head. "All right, Blair, but if you find out that love isn't always fair, don't be surprised. Remember it was Mitch who told you first." Their eyes met and held.

"I can't change who I am, or what I am, Mitch." Her tone was low and subdued. "I could never rush into marriage. It's too important a step to take in haste."

"What about love, Blair? Love never walks into a life, or strolls casually into a heart, does it? You didn't walk into my life, you rushed in. I love you and I am sure I love you. I want to marry you, that's how sure I am."

Before she could say anything in reply he leaned forward and lowered his mouth gently onto hers, and, feeling the soft pressure of his lips, she no longer needed to speak. Her arms closed around his neck. For a silent moment they drew back and faced each other.

She needed him madly, terribly. She knew the glowing embers inside her would turn to ash in that second if he pulled away from her. His eyes told her that was exactly what he was trying to do.

His head turned away from her and he started to move. Her arms tightened around his neck. "Going somewhere, Mr. Morgan?" she murmured.

He turned slowly back to face her, his eyes meeting hers in unwavering determination. "It isn't going to be this way, Blair. The next time we make love, you will be my wife. I respect your decision for more time."

His words slowed when her hands came from around his neck down to the front of his shirt, unfastening the one button. "Go on," she murmured. "I'm listening." Her hand moved inside the shirt, her fingers exploring the lean exposed flesh of his chest.

He inhaled deeply, but shakily. "I—" He moistened his lips. "I think in order to give your legal mind the time—"

Both hands moved lower, sliding up under his shirt. He reached down and grasped her hands through the soft material. "Blair, are you listening to me?"

Her head tilted back slightly and she grinned. "Of course I am. What do you think I'm doing, Mitch?" Her hands drew away from his, roaming downward to his waist. She felt the first slight shudder ripple through his body.

He cleared his throat, a quick lost sound. "If—if I can respect your decision for added time, then I think it's only fair that you respect mine to eliminate this aspect of our relationship until you're sure."

Her fingers nuzzled inside the waist of his snug jeans as she whispered, "I do respect your decision, but only a moment ago you told me love isn't fair and I also believe that. And that means, darling, that I'm going to get my time, but you probably aren't going to get your wish." She pressed back onto the sofa and pulled him over her. "Unless," she murmured, shifting so that she held him captive against her lower body. "Unless," she repeated in a whisper, entwining her legs around him, "you can kiss me now—and leave." She held his hard body tight against her, feeling his heart pacing wildly.

Flames burned away the determination in his glazed eyes. "You think you've won, don't you?" he moaned aloud.

"Oh, no," she whispered, catching his mouth in a slow, tormenting kiss, then releasing him slightly, her warm breath brushing his lips as she murmured, "Your evidence just didn't back up your case. But you may plead it again—tomorrow."

His face lowered, his lips intimately covering her mouth in a searching urgent sweep of passion. A forlorn cry rose softly in some distant part of her mind as she sensed the growing ache for him inside her. His ravishing kisses demanded all of her and she met that fierce demand until the entire room shook around them.

Her mouth opened and his tongue, hot with moist desire, stirred the deepest fires now flaming and raging, threatening to devour their very souls. His hands moved down her body, slowly removing her clothing.

Rising up slightly, she pulled the shirt over his head, dangling it from her hand a moment, then dropping it onto the floor. Her arms went around him and her mouth groaned against his chest, touched his ribs, buried into the firm smooth flesh at his waist. The cry inside her head grew in volume; the song of a tumultuous wind, a burning wind rising free.

His kisses were thick and fast on her soft flesh, moving down her neck, over her inflamed breasts, his lips and tongue invoking a cry to pass her lips. For a moment everything seemed still and motionless as they moved off together into the night.

Then he stood and slipped from the remainder of his clothes. With his body away from hers she lay shaking from cold, from fire; her head turned, her eyes reaching out to his body. Tapered fingers stroked his muscular thigh and moved slowly down to his knee, finding his skin cool to the warm touch of her hand. Ripples flexed in the muscles at her touch as her hand moved back along the inside of his leg.

Slowly he melted down beside her, the light blue of his eyes silver-glinted, his breathing soft, raspy groans. His hair fell limp across his forehead as he leaned over and circled her mouth with his tongue. He was powerless. She was powerless.

His fingers pressed softly into the flesh of her lower abdomen, moving down, pressing, touching, retreating, until the fire of hands caught and spread and carried them away in a whirl of flames. His body flattened hers, holding her there writhing beneath him as the cry in her head raised a piercing "Mitch!" from her throat.

Willingly he stifled the cry, his mouth covering her mouth, his body filling her body. He consumed her. Passion familiar, yet new, filled the vast space of darkness with the tense force of a gale until all cried, perished, and melted away into the night.

In utter quiet he lay breathlessly embracing her, an occasional shudder rippling the stillness they shared. She slowly opened one eye and peered at him, finding his eyes closed, his body motionless next to hers. A slow smile spread across her lips as she thought he looked like a mighty eagle.

"I feel your smile," he whispered hoarsely, his eyes remaining closed.

"Do you?" she murmured weakly, soft lips brushing his damp forehead. "I was just thinking you look like an eagle."

He muttered softly, "An eagle that has just flown into an electrical power line."

She ruffled his hair with her fingers. "Are you going to spend the night with me?"

Slowly he brought one arm from around her and raised up on one elbow, peering down into her face. "No, I'm not," he said with a polished sureness. "And I won't be spending the night with you until we're married."

Her mouth touched his chin and strayed along his throat. A sense of playfulness coursed through her. Completely relaxed, at ease with him, she smiled, enjoying the comfort of his body close to hers. "Mitch," she said suddenly, "are you finished with your overseas work?"

He stared thoughtfully into space, then turned his eyes to hers. "Uhmmm, I hope so. It's been a place of retreat for me, Blair. Somewhere I could live and work and keep my head intact."

"A place to delay the inevitable," she offered, placing her hand against his chest.

He smiled bleakly. "That, too, I suppose." He drew in a sharp breath. "I hated the thought of what I would be forced to do someday, but now I find it's all been done for me. I feel as if I've been given a new lease on life, thanks to you."

The playful sparkle left her eyes, replaced by a serious haze. She said gently, "Often, Mitch, I've

156

heard that justice is only an ideal, rarely achieved in reality. I have my doubts that your case came anywhere close to the ideal."

He caressed the side of her face with the back of his fingers. "Oh, I don't know about that assumption, Blair. I think maybe in this case we've seen justice in its truest form. I think maybe the scales may be tipped a bit in my favor, because the irony of ironies is that Charlotte unknowingly brought us together." He lowered his head and touched his lips to hers. "I need you in my life, Blair. I need to feel your love. For years I've been as barren as those deserts I've seen. I've felt like a desert."

She smiled lovingly. "A walking desert with a rich supply of love."

He kissed the tip of her nose. "Just under the surface, waiting to be tapped."

"I've tapped it," she whispered against his lips.

"Wildcatter," he teased, his lips pressing quick soft kisses along her throat.

CHAPTER TEN

When she walked into her office the next morning, smiling brightly, Lynn peered at her from behind the desk and said pleasantly, "Good morning, Blair. You've had a couple of early callers."

Reaching her door, Blair halted and looked back over her shoulder. "Anything urgent?"

"I don't think so," Lynn replied. "Sounded pretty routine. The messages and numbers are on your desk."

With a deep sigh and a dreamy smile Blair opened the door saying, "Fine. I'll get to them later."

"How was your weekend?" Lynn asked in a voice filled with laughter. Straightening in her chair, she looked quizzically at Blair.

"Just another weekend."

Still laughing, Lynn nodded knowingly. "Wayne must have changed his approach. It's obvious from

158

your expression something out of the ordinary happened this weekend."

Blair rolled her eyes. "He certainly did," she said, recalling the perplexing change that had taken place in Wayne's approach.

They both laughed and Blair went on into her office. Straightening the back of her skirt, she sat down behind her desk, swung around in the leather chair, and gazed out the window at the perfectly beautiful spring day. Maybe she had entered a fool's paradise, but she had walked in with her eyes wide open.

Watching a gorgeous redbird on a branch near the window, her eyes glowed as she sat in thoughtful contemplation. She followed the redbird as it jumped from limb to limb. On principle she had never been one to wish upon stars, or blowing out all the candles on a birthday cake. She counted on intelligence and determination to be the great grantor of her wishes. But watching the redbird she remembered her grandmother once telling her that if one wishes upon a redbird resting on a tree branch, the wish will be granted if the bird then flies upward, but if it flies downward to the ground, the wish will be denied.

She found herself placing a whispered plea on the bright red wings. "I want it to work for us. I love him so much. So very much. Let it work for us." She smiled wistfully at the bird and sat in spellbound silence waiting for it to take flight.

Unexpectedly the intercom sounded and she flipped around in her chair to press the button. Suddenly she jerked her head back to the window. The bird had flown away, but in which direction she had no idea.

Then when Lynn's voice penetrated the room with the announcement, "Charlotte Morgan to see you, Blair," she had the distinct impression it had nose-dived into the ground.

A moment passed before the door opened and Charlotte Morgan stepped inside, dressed in a hand-some coppery-red pantsuit. With an arrogant jaunt she moved across to the chair. The expression on her face was one that did not match her walk. She was worried.

Before she could speak, Blair held up one warning hand and said, "Mrs. Morgan, I must inform you that I am no longer in a position to represent you."

Charlotte's eyes blared. "What do you mean? You've been my attorney all along, since the beginning."

Blair hesitated, then, "I know. But I can no longer serve in that capacity. The situation has changed."

Interrupting, Charlotte exclaimed loudly, "You're damned right it has. That fool I was married to has completely lost his mind!" She moistened her lips nervously. "He isn't fighting me." Her eyes swept down to the floor. "He's given me everything!" She stopped, then looked up. "Something is terribly wrong!"

A grim silence fell between the two women. A moment passed and Blair said uneasily, "I don't think *he* gave you everything, I believe that decision was handed down by the judge based on the evidence presented in your case."

Charlotte looked at her with uncertainty. "I lied," she said simply. "I lied about it all."

Blair felt her mouth part with surprise. She felt the expression on her own face grow taut, felt the tightening of the flesh at the corners of her mouth. Presently she said, "I don't suppose it matters now." She touched a fallen strand of hair, pushing it back from near her eyebrow. "What's done is done," she said matter-of-factly.

Charlotte leaned forward. "No, what's done must be undone," she said, her face grim. "I fixed those papers, and a friend of mine notarized the signature. I told her Mitch had signed and she had no reason to doubt that it was his signature."

Blair closed her eyes momentarily and shook her head slightly. Now it was Mitch, not William or Bill. A terrible sinking began to seep inside her and she felt her heartbeat slow. In little more than a whisper she said accusingly, "You told me those signatures could undergo analysis to verify Mitch signed them."

Charlotte straightened, saying emphatically, "That's true. But what happened is that I took two of his cancelled checks, traced his signature through carbon on the papers, and then wrote over the carbon with indelible ink. Unless the carbon lines were detected, it would have passed as his."

Blair rubbed the bridge of her nose thoughtfully, feeling the flood of despair. "Why?" she whispered. "Why have you perjured yourself and involved me in this sordid travesty? Why have you lied?"

Charlotte's face flushed, and a rising tremble appeared in her voice. "To make him pay. I swore when he left me for that godforsaken country it would be for the last time!" Both sets of eyes met in a long stare. "I did it to show him what I could do. But I expected him to fight it." Her face went suddenly white. "I never intended for it to be final. I knew he could get the ruling overturned. I *expected* him to get the divorce set aside."

Blair closed her eyes and listened as Charlotte continued. "It's his fault. He drove me to do it. It's his fault for leaving me for months at the time. I'm his *wife!* But—but now there's some other woman in his life."

Blair opened her eyes. "The one you named in the suit? Marsha Partlow?" Her annoyance was growing and she couldn't stop it.

Charlotte replied in jerky words. "No—not Marsha. There was never anything between him and Marsha. I'm talking about someone else. I don't know her name. I only know that he's planning to marry her if we don't do something quick!"

"We!" Blair almost screeched. "We! Mrs. Morgan, I have removed myself from this entire matter. I told you clearly when you entered this room that I am finished with this case."

"You can't be. You presented this case and you will help me undo what I've done. I'm telling you as my attorney that I gave false testimony to that judge; the entire plea was nothing more than a succession of lies." She suddenly began to cry. "We've got to hurry, now, before Mitch has a suspicion of what I'm trying to do. I want to have the divorce set aside. You have no choice but to help me. You helped me when I lied. You must help me with the truth."

Blair had never felt so wretched. A moral obligation warred in fierce competition with her heart's obligation. At any other time in her life she would have seized an opportunity to set the record straight, but when she set this record straight the man she loved would again be married. Love wasn't fair. How invariably correct were his words.

"I only want to know if you're going to help me." Charlotte spoke glumly. "Because if you are, you need to get started—before it's too late."

Blair waited for a minute, then said, "Before I submit a plea to the court on your behalf, I think you must be made aware of the fact that—I am the woman."

Charlotte said nothing. Her gaze faltered and she swallowed quickly. Then she said in a rasp. "What!"

Blair inhaled deeply and repeated softly. "I am the woman."

Charlotte sat totally bewildered, a look of disbelief on her face. Then she caught her breath and said sharply, "You're lying!"

Trying to sound controlled, Blair returned one word, "No." She immediately caught the flicker of wildness in Charlotte's eyes. Then she said, "I'm not lying. There's a liar in this room, but it isn't me."

Frozen in the chair, Charlotte whispered with utter disbelief, "That isn't possible! Or ethical!"

Blair stared across, feigning a calmness she didn't feel. "It is both possible and ethical. And even more, it's true." A quick surge of feeling swept through her. "Now, I will go back to court with you and attempt to make right what's been done to Mitch, but before I can, or will, you have to understand that when it's over Mitch will be able to obtain his divorce whether or not you resist. There isn't a court or a judge anywhere in this country with so little consideration for his life—and his happiness, to prevent it. It's over. Whether or not you want to accept the fact, it's over."

Tears of rage filling her eyes, Charlotte jumped up. "I'll have you disbarred! You have breached a professional relationship! You have disclosed privileged information!"

"I have done no such thing!" Blair shot back angrily. "But do what you must. We all do."

Charlotte marched to the door, then turned and shook her head wildly. "You're fired!"

Blair's eyes flickered with startlement. "How kind of you," she muttered under her breath.

"And as for giving anything back to him—you can both forget it!"

Blair rose from her chair. "Aren't you ready to give up, Charlotte?" she asked as calmly as possible. "I'm not trying to advise you what to do, but haven't you had enough? What's to be gained now, regardless of what you do?"

Charlotte stared at her, her mouth twisting as she fought back tears. "You stole him!" she accused loudly. "Tell me, Miss Bennett, how does it feel to steal one of your client's husbands? Well, you're not going to get away with it." She seemed suddenly panicked. "You can't have him!"

Blair stared at her accusor. "You based your case on lies," she returned calmly. "Lies that backfired. So blame me for your failure if it makes you feel better, or even blame Mitch. I'm sure he won't mind." She hesitated and pointed one finger at the woman standing at her door, adding in a low dry voice, "But whatever you do, don't blame yourself. You were caught red-handed in your own little web of deceit, caught by the lies you spun." She turned around and glared out the window, saying over her shoulder, "There's nothing more we can say. Believe me, nothing."

She did not turn around when the door closed behind Charlotte. After a long time she sat back down at her desk, shaking her head slowly from side to side.

Still shaken by the encounter, Blair left the office at noon to meet Mitch for lunch. Entering the restaurant, she glanced around the dining room and saw him alone at a table, busily reading the menu. She stood for a moment, looking at him before moving slowly in the direction of his table. Apprehensively chewing her lower lip on the walk over, she smiled forlornly upon reaching his side.

He looked up from the menu, a warm grin covering his lips. Starting up from his chair, he said softly, "Hello there. I was wondering if you had forgotten me."

"Not yet, I haven't," she returned lightly, lowering herself into the chair opposite him.

"Not ever, will you?" he threw back glibly, again taking his seat. "Especially not after I tell you what's on the menu today." He opened the menu and said jokingly, "Special of the day—meat loaf, green beans, potatoes au gratin." He held up one finger, continuing dramatically. "Ah, before you fall out of your chair from sheer delight, that's not the best part. Listen to this, you have to make a high-level

165

decision about dessert. You may select either one scoop of vanilla ice cream or a slice of apple pie, but if you want both, there's a forty-cent extra charge."

"Mitch," she said seriously, interrupting his playfulness, "I need to talk to you."

He raised his brows, grinning quizzically. "Before or after the meat loaf?" He looked over at her and the sparkle began to leave the light blue irises. "What is it?" he asked somberly.

She shook her head and took a sip from her water glass. "I'd rather not discuss it here. Do you mind if we skip lunch?"

"No," he sighed worriedly. "I never cared for meat loaf or high-level dessert decisions. Where to?"

"Maybe we could walk back to my office. It's only a block or so from here."

A moment later outside on the sidewalk, he inhaled deeply. "What's happened?"

She gave him a troubled smile. "I don't really know." She paused, her eyes sweeping sideways down his lean muscular body clad in a pastel blue dress shirt open at the neck with the sleeves rolled up almost to his elbows, low-waisted deep blue slacks that molded nicely to his form with neat creases all the way down to shiny black loafers. A steady gaze rested on his profile a moment, then swept back to the sidewalk as she realized the clamor rising quickly inside her chest. She was surprised at how good she felt merely walking beside him.

His head turned and pale blue eyes looked down at her face. "I love you," he said in a soft whisper.

"And I love you," she returned in a voice equally as soft.

166

When they got to the office, she unlocked the door and pushed it open.

His face lightened. "No chaperon?" he whispered close to her ear.

She glanced back at him. "Lynn's out to lunch, but she will return promptly at one."

Closing the door behind him, he reached out and pulled her into his arms. "That's forty-five minutes. Do you have any idea what can be accomplished in forty-five minutes?" He chuckled.

They stood close together, eyes meeting in a searching hold. She could hear the humming in her head when she gave a shaky laugh. "Sometimes she gets back early."

"How early?" He smiled, a mischievous glint springing to life.

"Too early, particularly for what's on your mind." She placed both hands on his chest. "Besides, it's only noon and I still have half of a workday ahead of me."

His arms tightened around her slender body, pulling her so close that their bodies touched from waist to knees. "It's high noon," he said in a low, suggestive voice, his lips burrowing into the side of her head, his breath touching her ear. "Can you think of a better way to begin the second part of the day?"

Savoring his touch and the sound of his voice for a brief moment, she rested her head against his chest. Then she drew back and said firmly, "I may not think of a better way, but there are too many opposing factors."

"Name one," he murmured, leaning forward and kissing her ear tenderly.

"I'll do better than that, I'll name four. One, time is too short; two, Lynn's lunch hour will soon end; three, I have an appointment at one; and finally, if you'll look around you'll notice there are only chairs and desks and bookcases."

He sighed, then grinned down at her. "Why weren't you a psychiatrist?"

She laughed. "I should have been. We're all going to need one it seems before we get this mess straightened out," she confessed lightly.

He looked into her eyes again, his firm clasp around her body growing slack. "What is it now?"

She gave a long sigh and stared at him intently. "Mitch, there's a possibility that Charlotte will get the divorce set aside."

His face showed his surprise. "What!" he exclaimed. "That doesn't make any sense. Why would she do something like that?"

"Obviously because she's realized you aren't going to." Her eyes grew huge. "She was here this morning, and I'm not sure what you can expect from her."

His arms fell away completely and he stood shaking his head. "She came by my office this morning too. I shouldn't have said anything at all to her when she asked me my plans."

"What did you say?" Blair asked cautiously.

"Not that much." He smiled bleakly. "She wanted to know if I planned on trying to get the house back and in answer I handed her my set of keys to the house, the car, the lockbox. For God's sake, she wanted it. Why isn't she satisfied?" he asked angrily.

"I don't know," Blair whispered. "And I don't know what the court will do because I've never heard of this happening before. I suppose if she admits she perjured herself the judge will have no choice but to render the decree invalid." With a hint of exasperation she went on. "I know now that she didn't truly expect the divorce to stand. She did not expect you to step aside and allow her to keep it all. She expected you to fight her, Mitch."

He stood quiet, somber, then his mouth twisted into a strange smile. "Are you telling me, Blair, that regardless of what I do, I'm going to end up married to her again? Are you really telling me that?"

"Oh, Mitch, I wish I knew the answer, but I don't. The move is all hers. I think in her own way she loves you. She's just allowed it to become so distorted through the years. This action was merely to teach you a lesson." She raised sad eyes to his. "It was well planned from the beginning. She never intended for you to be free."

He struggled to control his fury. "Love is no excuse for what she's done. And you're wrong in assuming the move is hers—the move is ours. If you marry me, Blair, there isn't a judge in the world who would rescind that divorce." He took a step and clutched her arms. "The move is ours. Now, today. Either we take advantage of this time given to us by fate, or who knows when we'll ever find this time again."

She looked at his pale, forlorn face and felt the tears stirring to life. "I love you, Mitch. I do. But marrying you in haste isn't the answer. I don't know why she did what she did, except I do know that it must be resolved before you and I can begin a life together." She looked at him, pleading for understanding with her gaze. "I love you, Mitch, so much so I don't fear the time ahead. Whatever happens, I know my love for you will survive."

"Are you so sure, Blair?" he questioned, obviously troubled.

"Yes, I'm sure. I love you, Mitch. I'll always love you, regardless of what happens now." Her eyes swept over his face, her bluish-green irises glistening at his desperate gaze. "I will," she whispered in a choke, then, repeated, "I will."

His jaw tightened as he lowered his dark head and shook it slowly from side to side. "Someday it'll really be over, I suppose." He sighed deeply and added, "I hope."

That evening over dinner Mitch sat in a thoughtful silence, meeting Blair's eyes often, but saying nothing. Finally she asked, "Is something bothering you, Mitch?"

He smiled and said quietly, "I thought I would wait until after dinner to discuss it."

"Tell me now," she murmured.

"It has to do with Charlotte." He sighed. "I went to the house this afternoon to see her, to talk with her."

"And?"

His hands fell into his lap. "She's more frightened than anything, Blair. But I think she realized for the first time we can't go back. What's done is done."

She met his gaze with concern. "What is she going to do?"

"I'm not sure. We're probably going to have to get

together several more times to really clear the air so we can both get on with our lives."

She smiled and nodded.

"You have no misgivings?" Mitch inquired.

"No," she answered softly. And she didn't. If Mitch and Charlotte were talking again, everything could be worked out in due time.

CHAPTER ELEVEN

The next week was quiet, as was the following week. Then a month passed. Blair was amazed at the changes taking place inside her. Since she had known Mitch, especially since the first trying week, her life had smoothed out and taken new direction. Her clientele were much the same—disenchanted, disillusioned women, mostly young women who had reached the breaking points of a marriage. But for the first time in her entire career she had not accepted each client's word as the absolute truth. She had personally gained more respect for marriage and displayed this new respect often in the advice she dispensed to young women in unpleasant situations.

Loving Mitch had given a new dimension to her life, a dimension of tolerance and patience. And trust. She had never meant to be a short-sighted attorney, but she had been in many ways. It was a sobering thought to know she had helped end marriages that possibly could have been saved.

Mitch continued to fascinate her. She hoped he would never know what a hammerlock he had on her heart. They went out frequently, but the time she enjoyed most were the moments alone with him. Charlotte's plans remained a mystery, and the tension born of uncertainty heightened over the passing weeks.

Then on a warm balmy weekend night in June, she and Mitch were at his apartment in the process of dressing to go out to the movies and dinner. She had bathed and was adjusting her half slip when Mitch, dressed only in black trousers and socks walked up behind her and slid his arms around her waist. She looked up into the mirror and his blue eyes stared straight into hers in the reflection, a hypnotizing gaze, one that made her flush and bite her lower lip. His simplest touch made her weak and strong at the same time, made her knees weak and her heart strong.

His lips ruffled the side of her honey-blond hair as he kissed the top of her ear. "Do you love me?" he whispered.

Her eyes lighted up. "Of course not," she murmured jokingly. "Whatever made you think I did?"

His hands clenched together at her middle and he pressed closer to her back. His eyes studied her face in the mirror. He paused a long moment, then asked softly, "Have I taken the place of an apple in your life?"

She could not contain her smile as she gazed intently at him. She closed one eye and scrunched up one side of her face. "Don't you have any easy questions?"

He laughed strangely. "Just one." He hesitated. "If I should lose my wings, are you going to love me until I get them back?"

The light in her eyes dimmed and an expression of dismay fell on her face. "Mitch . . ." she breathed aloud in alarm. "She's done it?"

He grimaced. "Not yet. Next week. I meet with her and her attorney on Monday."

Blair cried indignantly, "Why? Why is she doing this! What is she trying to prove? What can she possibly gain by dragging it all through court again? Oh, Mitch, I'm so disappointed." She sighed. "I had hoped it was over. I was almost believing it was over. It's been weeks. And you've talked with her so many times."

"I know," he said reassuringly. "But, darling, in a way I'm glad, because I know when it ends this time it will truly end."

Determined dimples appeared in Blair's cheeks, put there by the tight line of her mouth. She shook her head slightly. "You know, I hoped that somewhere deep inside her that sweet girl you married ten years ago still existed—not for our sake, but for hers." She paused and went on. "It's tragic to know what she's doing to herself. It disturbs me so much to see someone vindictive to the extent of self-destruction. Why doesn't she stop? I thought all your talks had helped."

Strong fingers plied into the flesh of her stomach. "I've shared the same hope, Blair. I don't resent what she's doing anymore. I did at one time, but loving you doesn't give me room to harbor resentment for her. I don't know what the meeting is about. It caught me off-guard. I thought we had everything worked out. She seemed content the last time we talked." He looked distressed. "I may be a fool, but I believe in justice." He smiled suddenly. "I even believe in miracles."

She looked up at his smiling eyes in the mirror and hers misted in wonder. "I have seen few miracles, Mitch, none to be exact."

"Wait a minute, counsellor," he argued with a soft laugh. "You're a bright shining miracle, don't you know that? You appeared at the darkest time of my life. A miracle doesn't have to move a mountain to be a miracle. It just has to move a heart. Where's your little-girl faith?" he chided softly.

She turned in his arms and gazed at his face. "I suppose I lost it in my law books. Laws are what rule us, Mitch, not miracles."

"You are mistaken," he whispered, brushing the tip of her nose with his lips. "We make laws over those things that can be governed, but some things cannot be governed by man. What law can rule a heart, or stop a thought, or banish a love, or halt a miracle? Tell me, Miss Bennett, Attorney at Law."

She inclined her head slightly, leaning her forehead against his shoulder. "Mitch," she whispered, "you make it sound so uncomplicated, but this time next week you may find yourself again married to Charlotte. How can you be so optimistic knowing that?"

They stood embraced in silence a long moment.

"I'm sure, Blair," Mitch said in little more than a

175

whisper, "that whatever happens next week, you and I will find ourselves together at the end. I'm certain of it. However long it takes, whatever obstacles we must face, we'll do it together. And when it's over we'll be together. I love you, and that love is never going to die. Love only dies when people kill it. We aren't going to kill ours, not with doubt, suspicions, or jealousy. We're going to survive because that's the kind of love we share, a surviving love. And that's the best kind." He lifted her face, putting his hand beneath her chin, and their eyes held a minute.

Completely secure in his arms, she let her body sway with his slightest movements. She drew closer to him, aware of the depth of her love for him. It was more than a surviving love; it was a belonging love. She belonged to him. He belonged to her. And wherever they were together, they belonged. She had waited a long time for a love like this.

She buried her face against his chest and her arms went around him. He was warm and wonderful. She looked up at him with a half-smile. "I almost wish we had gone to the cabin instead of staying home this weekend," she whispered suddenly.

His eyes smiled at her. "For someone who liked mountains only from afar, you have certainly adjusted well to that cabin." His warm breath caressed her silky hair. "What is it about the place that intrigues you so, considering we've spent the past four weekends there?"

Her lips gently brushed his shoulder. "Oh, I don't know." Her lips continued downward with the lightest pressure along his chest. "I suppose that night on

176

the edge of the cliff changed my concept of the mountains."

Placing his hands on the sides of her face, he brought her gaze upward. "No matter what you say," he began jokingly, "it wasn't dangerous."

"I know that mountain climbers wouldn't have done it, not there."

Humor sparkled in his eyes. "It was there or never, or so I feared."

She laughed, her fingers squeezing into his back, then slowly traveling upward, sliding around his neck. She looked into his twinkling blue eyes. "Forgive me," she whispered, her face flushing brightly, "if I don't believe you, because I don't."

He placed the back of one hand on the side of her face and said softly, "Just as that was the last-chance ledge, this is the last chance for me to put on my shirt and you, your dress. That is, if we're going to get there in time to see the movie. You said you wanted to see it."

"I do." She smiled. "I really do want to see it, don't you?"

He nodded. "Sure I do." He gave his head a quick nod, adding, "More than anything."

Her eyes widened. "More than anything?" she repeated, raising her brows slightly and laughing softly. "It seems you neglected to tell your body." Her arms tightened around his neck and she moved closer, feeling the warmth of his skin against hers.

Her hands gently caressed the leanness of his neck and back. "I feel this is a time for options." Her fingers slid up his neck into his smooth damp hair.

"Let's talk options," he whispered, covering her

mouth with his in a devouring kiss that rocked her on her feet as they stood pressed to each other, toe to toe. Holding her tight, he released her mouth. "I have exercised my first option," he said, kissing one closed lid, then the other.

Slowly she pulled back in his arms, her hands moving down, seeking the waistband of his trousers, her fingers releasing the button. "My option is to make you neat. Black dress pants without a shirt is not at all becoming. So my suggestion is to either put on the shirt or take off the pants." Her hands moved inside the waistband, traveled around his slender middle, touching firm flesh, allowing the pants to slide slowly down until he stepped forward one step. Her fingertips brushed the lean rippling muscles of his thighs as she journeyed upward again to stand face to face with him. She smiled with love in her eyes.

He reached out, pulling his breath in sharply. "So much for the movie . . ." With charged fingers he loosened the clasp of her bra and pushed the straps from her shoulders, allowing it to drop to the floor, followed by the half slip.

Both undressed; they stood close, but not touching, eyes devouring each other. She smiled and uttered, "So much for dinner afterward."

A soft sound escaped him as he slowly brought her body against his. "God, you're beautiful, Blair."

He brought her into his arms and she whispered the last breathless words, "So much for the world around us."

An invisible, passionate force propelled her against him and she closed her eyes, feeling his lips tenderly brush her face, her eyelids, her cheeks, her nose, until at last their mouths blended together, her own trembling and parting to touch, to taste, to capture his seeking tongue.

His hands moved warm along her back from her shoulders to her hips, gentle strokes that brought a moaning gasp from her. Breaths grew thicker, the world grew darker beyond them, as though moon and stars had never existed. Clouds of passion swept in, taking away all dimensions of existence except the one they occupied in each other's arms. There was nothing beyond this time of need.

He drew her down to the bed and she wiped away the perspiration from his forehead with her fingertips in the moment before his lips crushed hers. Then slowly, languidly, his mouth moved from hers and his hot breath pierced the soft flesh of her neck, tracing a slow moist path to her breasts, which he tasted eagerly, building the pleasure, increasing the need until she could not bear the desire gripping her.

The clouds were parting and a pale light began shining through the maze of ecstasy. Delightedly her hands began sensuous new patterns along his skin, pressing him half-savagely until he lay mesmerized and rigid in the incredible oblivion they shared alone and together. Her arms circled his neck, clinging to him as though she were drowning in that one blinding unfathomable instant of bodies blending together.

He held her, crushing her and being crushed, both fallen prey to the singing winds of passion that blew them helplessly beyond the elements. Flaming colors flared behind eyelids closed tightly in rapture as they writhed and melted together in the completeness of their world. Everything grew very still except for the thin sounds of gasps flying from their mouths to be lost somewhere within the room.

Slowly she opened her eyes as the whirlwind died away completely in her mind. She peered at him through heavy lids and found his face blurred. With a little shake of her head the mist fell away and she could see his smile. His smile was a torrent of fresh air and cool water washing over her, making her feel more alive, more needed, more essential than she had ever felt before. She threw back her head and gasped aloud, "Do you have any idea how much I love you, Mitch?"

He roused himself, raising himself up on one elbow. His tongue stirred at her lips, bringing moisture to parched dryness before he spoke. "I don't know exactly how much, but I do know you love me more than you love movies or dinners."

She laughed softly. "I really did want to see that movie."

"I did too," he declared breathlessly. "Maybe someday we will. We'll catch it on the late show."

Her slender fingers caught his face and she pulled him back until lips met again.

CHAPTER TWELVE

Monday. A regular workday, but not regular by any stretch of the imagination. The morning had started in a frenzied disaster. She had burned the toast to a black crisp, been all thumbs trying to dress for work, and to make matters intolerable, had run out of gas on the drive into the office and had to leave her car and get a taxi.

The first session with a client had turned out horribly, the young woman leaving in tears because Blair refused to initiate the divorce papers prior to counseling. She felt like a blank piece of paper fate was about to write on. She knew she was being silly. Whatever the outcome between Mitch and Charlotte's meeting today, she and Mitch would eventually be together. Still, she was afraid.

A soft knock on the door and she looked up to see Lynn step inside saying, "The service station sent your car back, Blair, with a full tank of gas." She walked over and dropped the keys on the desk. "The attendant said to tell you when that little hand gets on the last black mark that means it's empty." Lynn laughed good-naturedly. "And I told him to kiss off, the last thing we needed on Monday was a smart-aleck gas station attendant. I'm not taking anything else from a smart-mouthed man. I've made up my mind on that."

Blair stared at her, and after a moment said vaguely, "Good."

Lynn's smile faded and her eyes searched Blair's face intently. She pursed her lips, then spoke in a low voice, "You didn't ask about my weekend, Blair, but in case you're interested, I ran away from home with the milkman, leaving Terry and the kids with no milk."

Blair looked up dully. "Oh, did you?" she replied absently, then suddenly her head jerked and her eyes widened. "You did what!" she exclaimed.

Lynn laughed. "Where is your mind today, Blair? You walked in like you were cloaked in a fog. I was just testing to see if you were paying attention. Obviously you weren't. What's the matter, or can't you say?"

Blair winced and felt her shoulders droop. "I've never felt so helpless in my entire life, Lynn. I mean, really helpless. My life is being decided this very moment and here I sit, powerless."

Lynn lowered herself into a chair and for a moment did not break the silence that fell between them. Finally she said, "It's the ex-wife, huh? What's she doing this time?"

Blair sighed and spoke with effort. "I only wish I

knew. I wish I had known what she was up to months ago when she first entered this office. I keep asking myself what will I do, what will I do if the divorce is nullified?"

They both heard the outside door open at the same time. Lynn rose from her chair and glanced at her watch. "I'd better see who that is. I suppose it's the mailman."

Blair watched her leave, then turned her attention back to the open file on her desk. Her eyes mechanically moved over the typewritten words.

The door suddenly opened again and Lynn stuck her head inside. "Special delivery for you." She smiled and pushed the door open wide.

For a moment her heart stopped utterly still. Mitch stood in the doorway looking steadily over at her. He was not smiling, his eyes were darkened and somber, his hair tumbled across his forehead as he stood motionless, the dark-colored suit neatly cloaking his fine body.

She immediately bit down on her bottom lip, her gaze going over him. He walked through the doorway, closing the door behind him. She could not analyze the look on his face. It was almost as if he wore no expression at all. She shivered inwardly, whispering, "Is it over?"

He looked blankly at her, then nodded his head once, then again. He walked over and sat down across from her. For a moment he was silent, then said simply, "She wasn't unreasonable. It went well, really." His eyes moved past her to the window and beyond. "She was more like the woman I married years ago." Slowly his eyes moved back to Blair.

"Maybe it took all this to get that woman back. But she's back, hopefully, to stay."

Blair could not understand or interpret the stirrings of emotions inside her. It was almost as if she could see the woman he had loved and married in the softness of his blue eyes. She could not even half-grasp what must have gone on inside that other attorney's office. All she could grasp was her general uneasiness, the signal of fear, of loss flashing through her. "Was the attorney with you?" she questioned in a whisper.

He shook his head. "Only part of the time. We met first with him, then alone, and then with him again at the end."

She followed his words, her heart twisting wildly inside her chest.

He straightened abruptly in his chair. "Do you want to know the details?"

She looked intently into his eyes, then said firmly, "Yes. Maybe not the details, but the outcome?" She added rapidly, "I want to know what to expect."

A slow smile started on his lips and spread outward. "The outcome is that I am free," he said quietly. "No more battles, no more squabbling. It's over. Now, would you like to kiss your free man, or are you going to continue to sit like a stone behind that desk?"

For a moment she didn't move. She watched him rise slowly to his feet, and then she leaped up from her chair, rounded the desk, and threw herself into his arms.

He stood holding her a long moment, one hand resting against the back of her hair. His lips brushed

184

her forehead. "At last she understands, Blair, that what we had once is gone. At first she didn't want to admit it, but today when we were alone in that room, that barrier she's had around her all these years began to crumble away."

Blair's eyes widened up at him, but she remained speechless.

"She understood there was nothing for us, that we truly didn't belong together, but by being apart we could begin living again. We had suffered the worst kind of existence together, a marriage without love. Nothing's worse than two people wasting each other's lives running and hiding from each other. That's all we've done for six years, and that's a long time to run and hide." He stopped talking and looked deeply into Blair's eyes. "I want her to love again, Blair. I do. I want her to be able to care for someone the way I care for you. I want her to be happy, as happy as I am this moment."

His head bent forward and he brushed her lips. "She's selling everything and going home to Texas. If she stays here, the past will haunt her, but there it'll all be new again. She tried to give me half of what she'd taken, but I didn't want it. I was thinking of how much I had already."

Tears glistened in Blair's eyes as he drew her closer and she felt the lean strength of his arms around her. "When you hold the world in your arms, it's damn greedy to ask for more, don't you think?"

She pulled away and smiled into his eyes. "I would never ask for more," she whispered, cradling his face in her palms and drawing his mouth to hers. She kissed him long and soundly, and when she released him a sparkle appeared in the depths of her eyes. "Except maybe a sofa in this office."

He laughed and squeezed her tighter to him, questioning in a low voice, "Is Wayne Fairfield the only jeweler in this town?"

She sighed. "Afraid so," she murmured, clinging to him.

He grinned mischievously, touching her face. "In that case, my darling, you'll probably be the only girl in the world who gets a sofa for the office put around her finger for an engagement ring."

She laughed, saying, "That'll be fine, just as long as the band is gold."

Nothing more was said as they both stood embracing, satisfied with the silence.

It was the most welcome feeling she had known and a pleased smile spread slowly across her lips. She had not truly believed this moment would arrive, not deep in her heart had she truly believed it.

Cradling her head against his neck, she closed her eyes, enjoying his touch, loving him more than words could say. They were all free now. At last.

LOOK FOR NEXT MONTH'S
CANDLELIGHT ECSTASY ROMANCES ®

Candlelight Ecstasy Romances

"THE MOST ROMANTIC NOVEL SINCE LOVE STORY"
—Good Housekeeping

Change of Heart

SALLY MANDEL

Once in a long while, a story is so bursting with tenderness that its charm is irresistible.

That story is Sharlie and Brian's story, Change of Heart— a love story for a lifetime.

$2.95